BARBARIAN'S HOPE

A SCIFI ALIEN ROMANCE

RUBY DIXON

RUBY DIXON

BARBARIAN'S HOPE

Seasons ago, I resonated to the quietest of tribesmates, a male content to love me from afar while I was the center of attention. We could have been happy. Despite our differences, I loved him and he loved me.

But then a terrible thing happened...and my world was never the same again.

Now resonance is giving us a second chance, but...I'm afraid. What if what I have with my mate is too broken to be fixed? What if there's no hope left for us at all?

1

ASHA

When I agreed to let Farli be my cave mate, I did not think things through.

I roll over in my furs, rubbing my face. It's early. My breath fogs in the darkness and the fire is nothing but embers. The howse is dark, and I'm not sure what woke me up.

Then something noses at my mane.

I shriek and sit up in bed, swatting at my mane. My head bangs into that of the dvisti, and it bleats, scurrying away, its hooves clacking on the stones.

"What? What is it?" Farli asks sleepily.

"Your pet was trying to eat my braid again," I bite out, running my hands over my hair. For some reason, Cham-pee finds my hair tasty and this is the third time in the last handful of days he has attempted to nibble on it.

She chuckles, which does not help my mood. "He thinks it's one of the braids of straw I've made for him." She gets up and I see her face in the shadows as she heads over to the storage bins. She pulls out a thick braid of straw and offers it to the dvisti. "He's just hungry, aren't you, little one?"

"He smells," I say with a scowl. "And he relieves himself on the floor."

"It's ready-made fuel," Farli tells me, unruffled by my anger. "No gathering needed." She gives her pet a hug, then wanders back to her bed. "He's harmless. Just hide your braid."

I snort and pull the covers back over my head, but I can't go back to sleep. The dvisti is chewing noisily, his large teeth grinding. It sounds overloud in the small howse and makes me toss and turn. I might as well get up. Somewhere out in the vee-lage, a kit cries.

My skin prickles with awareness and I think of my own little Hashala. Her cries were so weak, not the strong, healthy wails of the kits in the vee-lage now. I remember holding her in my arms, no bigger than my hand, and wishing my own strength into her small body. Anything to save her.

It did not work. Nothing ever worked. She died before a khui could even light her eyes.

I reach under my pillow and pull out her small tunic. It has lost her scent, but I still like to close my eyes and hold it close, imagining that it is her. Imagining that she lives yet again and my mate smiles at me and my kit nurses from my teats and we are a family. We are whole.

The kit cries again in the distance, and I sit up, putting on my tunic. I cannot sleep, and the sound of the crying tells me that there is another mother somewhere in the vee-lage that cannot sleep, either. Perhaps she will need help. Lately the only thing to rouse me from my bed is the thought of holding one of the many kits that fill our tribe with such hope and joy.

Seeing so many kits in the tribe is both the most wonderful thing...and the most difficult.

I slip on my boots as Farli rolls over in her furs, going back to sleep. The dvisti just chews placidly and watches me as I walk past. Sometimes I think it would be better if I had a howse of my own, but it would be very lonely. I do not think I want that.

I emerge from my small howse and head toward the center of the vee-lage. It is brisk today, a bit of snow falling. The sky is dark with storms, yet not much falls down below in our protected valley. The wind howls loudly above, which means that the hunters will be staying in this day. This also means that because their mates are home, many of the women will not be gathering by the main fire to exchange stories and let others hold their kits. They will be snuggled in their furs with their mates.

I am envious of the image this forms in my mind. There is nothing I would like more than a little family to fuss over at my own fire. Kits to hold close and spoil. A mate whose smiles promise wonderful things.

This is not for me, though. I have no living kits, nor do I think I will ever have one again. My mate has abandoned me. Everything I have ever wanted is out of my reach.

But life must go on, and it seems that this morning I cannot spend my time in my furs, sleeping. Not with that horrid dvisti trying to snack on my mane. I smooth a hand over one of my braids as if to double-check them, and make my way toward the center of the vee-lage, toward the big building the others are calling the long-howse. In it is the central fire and the bathing pool. If others are about today, they will be there.

As I walk down the main path, I see people climbing onto the walls of one of the small howses, straightening one of the hide covers. A teepee top, the humans call it. Since the howses have no lids, great hide covers have been constructed and vaulted over the top of each of the howses to allow smoke from fires to vent out and for the light snows that fall into the gorge to trickle harmlessly down the sloping sides. Each howse requires a very large hide to cover it, which means several are stitched together and fitted over the frame. It is a task that requires many hands working together.

I should not be surprised to see my once-mate there, but I am.

Hemalo has his back to me, his tail flicking as he smooths hide over one of the long bones that props up the frame. I recognize his body instantly, the graceful motion of his shoulders as he reaches over and points at the far end of the structure. "Tighten your corner, Kashrem. We need to pull taut."

I pause to watch them work. Kashrem and Hemalo are the tribe's most experienced leather-workers, so it is natural that they should take charge of roofing each of the howses. He is in his element, confidence and knowledge in his stance, and enthusiasm in his smooth, rolling voice that still sends ripples right down to my tail when he speaks.

I should hate him. I should hate him for abandoning me. For giving up on me as I work through my grief. But I do not hate him. Instead, all I feel is a bone-deep ache that seems to devour from within.

He is happy, my once-mate. Hemalo has always loved to feel needed, and that is something I have not been able to give him. This move to the new vee-lage, the chance to work his skills and be important to the tribe—all of it is wonderful for him. For once, it is Hemalo that is needed and in demand, and Asha who is unimportant.

I cross my arms over my chest, curious at how uneasy that makes me feel. In my mind, I am very different from the Asha I used to be. The one that flirted with all the males of the tribe and who went from pleasure-mate to pleasure-mate, just because she could. Just because I was one of two young females in the tribe and all the strong hunters wanted my attention. Then, all I wanted was to be the center of attention.

Now, the thought makes me tired.

"Grab the cords," Hemalo instructs, and I watch as Taushen and Ereven move around the far side of the howse, and the roof pitches even higher. "Just like that," Hemalo tells them. "Good job."

"Ho, Asha," Taushen calls out. "Do you come here to help?"

All of the workers stop, but my gaze is on Hemalo. He stiffens, his tail flicking, and he turns slowly to look at me. There is sorrow and apology in his eyes. It makes me angry.

"No," I say, keeping my voice tart. "I was looking to see who was making so much noise that they would rouse good people from their sleep." Not that I was asleep, but they do not need to know that. "It is early."

"Ah, but if we wait until you are awake and out of the furs, we could be waiting a very long time," Ereven calls out.

I ignore his jibe.

Hemalo shoots Ereven a look. "My apologies," my once-mate says in his low, thrumming voice. "We will be quieter."

"Do as you like." I shrug as if it does not matter to me. It feels strange to stand apart from him as if we are merely tribesmates and not once-mates. I cannot be easy around him, and judging by the tense set of his shoulders, he feels the same about me.

Nothing is simple between us. I hate that, even though I know it is my fault as much as his.

The males continue to watch me, as if waiting for something. I shrug and move on, as if I am unaffected. The truth is, being this near Hemalo bothers me, like an itch I cannot scratch. Things are wrong between us, and I can feel the hot eyes of the others as they watch us both, waiting for one of us to blow up at the other. Waiting for us to fight and snarl like we always have in the past.

I am not interested in that, though. I am just...tired. I want to move on.

I head toward the long-howse, and the closer I get, I smell something cooking over the fire. Someone is there, at least. I hurry in to get out of the wind—one of the things I am not quite used to despite several moons of living in the vee-lage. It still feels very open to me, very exposed. Perhaps it always will. The humans love it, though. They say it feels more like home to them.

I step into the long-howse, and warmth hits me. This room is drowsy-warm and humid, thanks to the warm pool at the center. The lid of the long-howse is cleverly rigged as multiple skins that can be dragged closed or pulled open, depending on the weather. Most days it is left open because the walls keep the worst of the wind out, and everyone likes the sunlight. It is so warm here that Tee-fah-ni has potted several fruit plants and keeps them in the direct sunlight, hoping they will grow. In one corner, there are drying racks of roots and herbs, and another of meat.

Stay-see is by the fire, and No-rah is with her, both of her kits' baskets at her feet. I feel my spirits lift at the sight of them—No-rah always needs help with her twins, and I am glad to hold them. "Good morning."

"Hi, Asha. We were just sitting down to have some eggs." No-rah beams a bright smile at me. "You hungry?"

"I will eat." I sit down next to No-rah while Stay-see pushes a lumpy yellow paste around in her skillet over the fire. I personally do not like the taste—or the thought—of the eggs. The humans love them, but the sa-khui are revolted by the taste and texture and the fact that they are uncooked young. We revere the act of life, so it seems horrible to me to eat dirtbeaks before they hatch from the shell...but it is food, and the stores are lean. So I will eat eggs and smile through gritted teeth as I do so.

One of the twins starts to snuffle and cry, and I look over at No-rah. "May I?"

"Please do." She gives me a tired smile. "They were up all night fussing." No-rah stifles a yawn.

I pick up one of the twins—Ah-nah. I can tell her apart from her sister because of the way her bright yellow mane sticks up. Her 'cow-lick,' as the humans call it, makes her tufts stick up toward her brow, whereas El-sah has a smooth mane. If I have to be particular, Ah-nah is my favorite of the two. She is a little fussier than her calm twin, a little less settled. I can relate to that.

I hold her close, inhaling her sweet kit scent. She cries a little but quiets when I tuck her against my neck and I stroke her small head. My kit would have been like this. Not with the yellow mane or the pale, pale blue skin, but my Hashala would have filled out like Ah-nah if given time. Her little fingers would curl around my larger one, and she would gurgle and make happy noises and tug on my braid when she got excited, like Ah-nah is right now. My heart squeezes painfully.

Sometimes I pretend that No-rah is tired of two kits and will give me one. It is a foolish hope, but one that lives in my head anyhow. Why should one female have two when I have none? But that is not how life works, and my arms must be empty while No-rah's overflow.

Stay-see serves up the eggs, and she and No-rah tuck into the food with enthusiasm. I choke down a few bites but spend most of my time cuddling the kit as the two humans chatter about the weather, their mates, and Stay-see's ever-increasing stash of frozen eggs.

As the humans talk, Claire wanders over. "I smell eggs. Are there any left?" She rubs her lightly rounded stomach, the kit she is carrying now starting to show even though it will not be born until well after the brutal season is over.

"I can make more," Stay-see tells her. "Not sleeping in today?"

Claire shakes her head and sits down by the fire, smiling a greeting at me. "Sleep? Not with the men shouting instructions at each other while I'm in my furs. But at least the leak in the roof will be fixed. Hemalo knew exactly what the problem was. Something about how the leather was treated, so they removed the piece that was dripping meltwater and are replacing it."

The humans glance over at me, as if expecting me to say something since my once-mate was brought up. I remain silent, content to hold Ah-nah. I do not want to leave and return to my howse. Not when there are kits here by the fire and I have nothing waiting for me at home.

Stay-see cracks another egg over her skillet and then begins to stir. "So, did you talk to Georgie?" She asks Claire.

"It's a go," Claire says happily, settling into her seat and sliding her hands over her rounded belly. "She thinks another holiday will help perk everyone up."

No-rah looks excited. "I would love that. I think it's nice to have the guys home on bad weather days, but I know they get restless when too many of them string together. Just the other day it snowed so hard that the hunters were stuck in the village for five days straight, and I thought Dagesh would climb the walls, he was so restless. By the time the weather cleared I was ready to shove him out the door." She chuckles.

I smile faintly. "It is just part of the brutal season. We endure the slow days and get as much as we can get done on the good weather days." I shrug. I would not mind a day that was so busy myself. Without a mate or kit at my hearth, I have too much free time. I am no huntress, like Leezh or some of the other humans that are learning.

All I have ever wanted is to be a mother.

"So what is the plan?" Stay-see asks as she cracks another egg over the skillet and begins to swirl it around with her bone spoon. "Another mashup of holidays like last time?"

Claire clasps her hands together under her chin. "I was thinking we could do twelve days of Christmas. Except, not Christmas," she amends, giving No-rah an apologetic look. "I know you're Jewish."

No-rah waves a hand. "It's not about religion here, anyhow. It's about community. We can call it whatever."

"Well, I was talking to Ariana," Claire continues. "She said that in medieval times they celebrated twelve days of Christmas overall. It was called Epiphany."

"Twelve days of Christmas," Stay-see murmurs, nodding.

"Right. I thought that might be something fun we could do—take the holiday and spread it out over several days so we can make the most out of it." She looks over at me. "What do you think, Asha?"

I am being asked? I shrug. "Everyone enjoyed the last haw-lee-deh." Except me, but there are few things I enjoy anymore. I hold Ah-nah closer and sniff her sweet-smelling mane again, lost in her scent. "If anyone wishes to celebrate, I will be happy to watch their kits." That will give me more joy than the foot-and-ball game they played last time there was a haw-lee-deh.

"But maybe we can think of ways to bring in sa-khui customs instead of just purely human ones," Claire tells me. "Surely there are games you play, or foods you eat to celebrate. You must have customs that I'm not thinking of, yes?"

I shrug.

"I remember the head-butting thing from last year," Stay-see says with a shudder. "Maybe we skip that part."

"Eeek, I remember that, too." Claire looks worried.

"It is a game," I tell them, amused at how it bothers the humans. Head-butts between hunters are nothing but showing off for females. It does not hurt them, because their great horns protect their hard skulls. But I suppose there are no human females to show off for this time.

"Maybe we need different games. Like Secret Santa."

"Oh my god, I love Secret Santa!" Stay-see stirs the eggs vigorously and gives Claire an excited look. "We should totally do that!"

"San-tuh?" I echo. "It is a food? Better than eggs?" I eye my half-eaten plate of yellow fluff. It is going to take all that I have to choke it down.

The humans laugh. No-rah explains, "Santa is Santa Claus. It's a Christmas tradition. He's a man—"

"A jolly old elf," Claire breaks in.

"Right," No-rah continues. "And he slides down the chimney and brings gifts to all the boys and girls who have been good all year...um, season."

"Chim-nee?" I ask.

"The smoke hole in the ceiling. Kinda."

I frown at this thought, even as Ah-nah grabs one of my braids and pulls hard. "This fat man falls into your fire with your gifts? How is that a reward?"

Claire giggles. "If you're not good, he brings you coal. Fire fuel."

"Fire fuel is useful," I point out. "I shall be bad and someone will do my chores for me. I like this custom."

All three women laugh again. "That's not how it works, Asha. You can't be deliberately naughty," Stay-see says, grinning. "Though I guess you can if you want to. And I guess fuel isn't that bad of a gift, all things considered. I guess we'd have to tweak things a bit for Not-Hoth holidays."

"It's a work in progress," Claire agrees with a nod. "I'm going to make a list with some coal and one of the skins and see what I can come up with. Maybe we can come up with one event a day and spread things out."

"Don't forget the food. I like the food," Stay-see tells her.

Ah-nah makes an unhappy noise and then begins to cry. I bounce her, trying to soothe her unhappiness, but then her sister El-sah begins to wail, and then both twins are howling. No-rah grimaces and takes Ah-nah from me, opening her tunic to nurse. "So much for quiet time in the morning."

"Shall I hold El-sah?" I ask. I itch to hug one of the weeping kits to my breast and soothe it. My heart longs so much for a kit of my own. Oh, my sweet little Hashala. I miss her every day.

"It's okay. I can nurse them both at once," No-rah says and expertly juggles her second child to her other breast. "I'm getting to be a pro at this."

Stay-see serves a pile of eggs to Claire, and the two women continue to talk about the haw-lee-deh and their human customs. I choke down the rest of my food, since times are lean and food is not to be wasted, even if it tastes poor. I feel very alone again, and sad. I finish my plate and get to my feet.

"Leaving, Asha?" No-rah looks up at me. She means well, but she cannot understand how jealous I am of her happiness.

I simply nod. "Tired," I say, and hate that my voice is flat and angry. I am not truly sleepy, but my furs are a refuge from the world, and right now I just want to crawl into them and forget for a few hours again. I leave the humans' fire and head back to my howse. A few more people are waking up and moving about their day. Leezh and her mate are walking through the center of the vee-lage, lost in conversation. Raahosh holds their little daughter close and nods at his mate's words. In the distance, I can hear Cashol and Mehgann laughing together. So many kits. So many happy families.

I duck into my howse, glad to find it dark and silent. The dvisti is near my side of the howse, and I shoo it away. Stupid animal. I climb into my furs and pull out Hashala's little tunic. I bring it to my nose and sniff it, but it has lost the kit-scent that perfumes Ah-nah's mane.

"Back to bed?" Farli asks, sleepy. "Is there food at the fire?"

"Eggs," I say flatly. "Lots of eggs."

She makes a noise of dismay.

I remain silent, hoping she will leave and let me be. But Farli sits up in her furs and smacks her lips, yawning, oblivious to my mood. She pets her dvisti for a time and seems to be in no hurry to leave. I roll over in my blankets, presenting her with my back. As I do, I think. Farli is a lot like me. Maylak, Farli and I are the only sa-khui young females in our tribe. There is old Kemli and Sevvah, but neither is close in age to me. Maylak was always my rival...and she now has everything I ever wanted: a happy mate, a secure place in the tribe, and two kits. The male hunters that should have been falling over themselves to court Farli are now mated to humans, and the humans tend to stick together. They keep human customs and talk of human things, and sometimes it makes me feel very isolated in my own tribe. I am not the stranger, and yet...I no longer fit in with my own people.

I roll onto my back and look over at Farli again. She is braiding her long mane in lazy, slow motions, yawning. "Do you ever feel like an outsider, Farli?"

She gives me a puzzled look. "An outsider?"

"Because of the humans?"

Her head tilts. "Should I?"

I sigh. Perhaps it is just me that is discontent. "Never mind. Go and talk to Stay-see and Claire. They are discussing another No Poison Day."

That gets her attention. She makes an excited sound and bounds out of her furs. I hear the dvisti dancing around her as she dresses, and then a moment later, they are both gone.

Quiet at last. I hug Hashala's little tunic to my breast and try to go back to sleep.

2

HEMALO

"You have my thanks," Ereven tells me with a clap on my shoulder. He gazes up at the new cover for his howse, pleased. "I do not want to wake up in the middle of the night with Claire soaking wet again. My mate is far too fragile for that."

I nod absently. Ereven is a good hunter, but it is clear that his thoughts lately are focused solely on his quiet mate. It is a tricky thing to discuss with a man that has recently parted ways with his own mate, but Ereven has no malice in his words or thoughts. He is just happy and wants to share his happiness. "It is no problem. The fix was an easy one once we pulled the leather cover off the frame."

"You must let me give you my next set of skins as a show of thanks," he tells me. "What do you need? Dvisti? Snowcat? Ask and it shall be yours."

"Save them for your mate and your new kit. I have more skins than hours in the day to work them."

"Then you must eat with us this day," he continues. "Though I must warn you that because she is carrying, my mate likes her food charred." He makes a face but looks pleased at the thought regardless.

I raise a hand in protest. "I have dried food. I am fine." I would rather eat smoke-dried meat than choke down a mouthful of the hot, burnt flesh the humans are so fond of. "Feed your mate, not me."

He grins. "All right, but the next fresh kill I have, it shall be yours."

I nod absently at him, studying my work. I am pleased with how the cover turned out. With each howse, Kashrem and I have gotten better with creating the covers for each one. The seams on this howse are tight and invisible. The edges are pulled taut with the stone, and not even a breeze will be able to make it through to bother Ereven's fragile human mate. We have done good work this day, and I am proud. It is not necessary for Ereven to repay me, however. I would do the same for any tribesmate. "If you have extra meat, perhaps bring it to Asha," I tell him, thinking of my glimpse of my once-mate from earlier.

She looks thin, my Asha, her eyes hollow with grief. I still want to comfort her, though I know she will not allow it. She is proud, and she struggles. Our once-mating was not healthy, and I ended it because our misery together felt worse than being apart. I miss her. She is my heart, but on that awful day seasons ago, she lost our daughter.

I lost my mate and kit both.

I know she has never wanted to be mated to me. I am not flashy, like Harrec, or easy with words like Aehako. I am a simple male…but I have always loved Asha, even when she did not know I existed. I will continue to love her, even though we are apart. And I will always care for her.

Thinking of the mate I have lost sours my mood. I nod a goodbye at Ereven and head back toward the howse I share with the other hunters. It is on the far end of the vee-lage, since we are all sa-khui and do not suffer from the cold as the humans do. We keep quarters together to save on resources, and most days the other hunters are out on the trails, which means I am alone in the howse. On bad weather days, when everyone remains in the vee-lage, however, it gets cramped. Today is one of those days. Harrec, Taushen, Bek, and Warrek are in the small hut. Bek is busy carving something, his tools spread out around him. Harrec is lazing in his furs, chatting with Taushen as the other works on sharpening his spears. Warrek works on fishing nets, and between all of them, there is no room for me to spread out hides and work on my own projects. Annoyed at this, I grab a few rolls of hide and my pots and take them across the cobbled road to one of the empty howses with no lid. Here, it is colder, but I can spread out.

And here, I will have no one to disturb my thoughts.

Many of the tribe are not fond of making leather. It is a necessary task, but one that few enjoy. It is messy, hard work that requires scraping the hide over and over again, and even fewer have the patience to make truly soft, supple leather. I enjoy it, though. I like the chance to create soft, beautiful, functional things for my tribe. I can hunt and I can fish, but I am truly good at making leather. I do not mind getting my hands dirty or spending hours rubbing brains and fat onto the leather. It allows me to think.

Lately I have needed to think quite a bit.

I roll out the hides, spreading them on the stone surface. It is hard on the knees but good for making hides, and I set my pots down and remove the lid off of one. The hide I am going to start with today is a snowcat hide. They are smaller than dvisti, but the resulting leather is as soft and delicate as a kit's backside. This particular piece is flawless, and I have scraped it clean on both sides. If I do this right, it will make a piece of clothing that will be the pride of its owner. I picture my Asha, lovely and proud, in a new hood or perhaps a tunic made of this particular piece. I will cure it and dye it for her and make her something beautiful to wear. Perhaps that would make her smile again. I like the thought and get to work.

My hands smooth over the hide. It is thick right now, and inflexible. It has been de-furred and de-fleshed, but it needs more work before it can be worn. I take out my framing materials and lash the frame together, then stretch the hide over it until it is taut, like a drum. I head to the bathing pool and use the pump that spits out hot water, filling one of my pots before returning to the hut. Once back, I tug another small bone pot over to my side and bring out the frozen brain of the snowcat. It has turned to a block of ice while waiting to be used, and I dunk it in the hot water, waiting for it to thaw. When it does, I break it up in the water and work the mix with my hands until it forms a thick, gooey paste. Then I take a handful of the paste and begin to slowly rub it into one corner of the hide.

Working during the brutal season means that hides take twice as long to cure. In the warmer season, back when we had the cave, I would slather the entire hide with brains, let it sit out until the solution soaked into the leather, and then work on softening it. Because it is so cold, I cannot leave the brain-mash out on the hide or else it will freeze instead of soaking in. So I take small handfuls and rub over a small portion of the hide, moving my hands over it repeatedly to let the warmth of my body keep the solution from freezing. It means I must go that much slower, but that means my thoughts can turn inward, to Asha.

I know she is troubled. I know she hungers for another kit. I have seen the starved, desperate looks she gives the human females, especially No-rah, who has two kits. She will not do anything to harm them, of course, but I know it cannot be easy for her. Back before the humans arrived, it was just Maylak she envied. Now it seems like every female of childbearing age is pregnant or has a kit under her arm, and my poor mate suffers because of it. She was getting better before the humans arrived, I think. But once the first kit was born, she retreated. With every new kit born to a happy couple, she retreats a bit further.

And there is nothing I can do. I would give her anything that would make her smile. Anything that would rid her of her pain. But I can do nothing. She will not accept my love, so I gave up on trying.

I do not resent Asha. I try not to resent the humans, though sometimes it is hard. They are kind females, and they do not mean to harm her. It is just that their presence is a dagger in my mate's heart...and I will not let anything harm her if I can help it. So I keep to myself and let others fawn over the humans.

Let them be pleased with their pale, strange mates and their flat faces. I have the most beautiful female in the tribe, whose vibrant blue skin and laughing eyes are the most spectacular thing a male could see.

And...I gave her up.

Disgusted and miserable at my own thoughts, I slap another handful of brain-mash onto the leather and rub it even harder, taking my frustrations out on it.

3

CLAIRE

I'm utterly focused on holidays and Christmas all day. Even though I volunteered to organize things, it still feels like a massive undertaking, and I want to make sure everyone enjoys the holiday. It'll be spread out over several days, of course, because that means we can get a reprieve from the endless snow and boredom of the brutal season.

We'll need food, because no holiday celebration is complete without a feast, but we'll have to be mindful of tight supply stores.

We'll have gifts, because every holiday involves gifts, and we'll need to make sure everyone is included and feels like they can participate. We'll have games and decorations so everyone can share in the fun.

And I can't make things too complicated, because then people will just get confused. So many human customs don't translate over to sa-khui. I still remember from our last holiday and the fact that the tribe couldn't figure out what mistletoe was used for. Hunters ended up giving their mates piles of leaves, expecting kisses for gifts of 'not poison.' In fact, everyone I've chatted with so far has referred to our holiday as 'No Poison Day' instead of Unity Day, like had originally been suggested.

I sit by my fire and make notes on a tough, pale hide with a bit of charcoal. I want to make sure I get everything right, and I want to make sure I don't forget a thing, so I need lists. I wish I had paper, but coal and hide must do. I first make a list of all the ideas from all the holidays I can think of and write them out. Easter egg hunts. Secret Santa. Valentine's Day and cards for your sweetheart. Heck, New Year's and kisses. Since No Poison Day is a mashup of everything, as long as we make things fun, it doesn't matter if it's a Halloween tradition or a Christmas one, because the sa-khui will be none the wiser and the humans just want to enjoy themselves.

Secret Santa is a good one to start with, I think. We can have everyone in the tribe pull names and be assigned a 'secret' person to give gifts to. Everyone will enjoy that, and the act of making gifts as well as giving them should be fun. I pull out a second hide and start writing out names. Someone will have to run things, and I can do it. It means I'll be in charge of the rules and making sure everyone plays, but if I'm going to have things running smoothly, I need to take control of it myself and I need to make sure no one is forgotten. I still remember last year, when everyone was being showered with gifts and poor Josie only got one from Liz, and how guilty I'd felt that I hadn't thought to give Josie a gift myself. I won't let that happen again. Everyone's going to share in the fun. So I write. I list each person's house and then everyone living there. I'm going to have to chat with each person individually to make sure everyone's clear on the rules. It might even take me a few days just to get everyone squared, so some of the other 'holiday' fun things will need to be easy. A feast day. A football day. A decorating day. A—

I'm so caught up in my plans for the holiday that I almost miss my baby's first kick. My stomach flutters, and I think it's gas, but when something smacks against my insides again, I gasp and sit upright, clutching my stomach.

"What is it? Are you well?" Ereven moves to my side, shoving away the skins I've been scribbling notes on. The look on his face is one of concern. "Shall I get the healer?"

"I think the baby kicked!" I beam a smile of wonder at him. "It's incredible." My stomach's been rounding out steadily for the last month, but I haven't felt more than the occasional flutter that made me wonder if it was a kick or just my imagination. What I just felt? That was most firmly a hello from my insides.

My mate's face lights up, and he shoves his tangled hair behind his ears, leaning in. His hands reverently touch my stomach, moving over the layers of furs I'm wearing. "You are sure?"

"Positive. Maybe he'll do it again." We've been calling the baby a 'he' just to have a gender, but something in my gut tells me I'm not wrong. I think it's a boy, and I hope he's as handsome and kind as his daddy.

Ereven waits, crouching low next to me. He keeps his hands on my belly, and he's so still, his gaze so intent, that I want to laugh partially out of joy and partially out of the absurdity of the moment. But then it happens again, and the sheer happiness and wonder on his face makes me want to weep. I've been doing a lot of that lately. "I felt it," he whispers. "Do you think he is trying to talk to us?"

"I think he's just restless," I say softly, sniffing back my emotions.

A slow smile curves Ereven's mouth. "He is not the only one." He leans in and speaks to my stomach, as if the baby can hear. "Your father wants to go out and hunt to feed your mother, but the weather does not permit it."

"Guess you'll just have to stay in with me," I tease. Like it's a chore to be snuggled in our little house together, especially now that the roof has been fixed. I don't mind the lazy days when the weather is bleak and awful and that means the hunters stay in. I like those, because it means we get to sleep late and cuddle, and it means I get to spend the entire day talking to Ereven about nothing at all and just enjoying his company. It's certainly not the worst way to spend the time.

He smiles at me, and I feel warm and good inside. My life is so wonderful with Ereven. He's so perfect for me in every way. His confidence in me makes me stronger, mentally. He gives me courage. I don't hide away any longer—now I do my best to take part in the tribe and participate every day. I feel like I'm making up for lost time. Heck, sometimes I feel like a different, better person. It's all thanks to him.

The baby kicks again, and Ereven sucks in a breath.

"You felt it?" I say with a laugh.

"I did." His voice is soft with awe. "He is strong."

"Like his father."

He brushes at my furs. "He is also covered in ash. Why do you have soot all over you, my mate?"

I do? I dust my fingers over my clothing, just now noticing the dark smears all over my gray leathers. Of course, that just makes things worse, and I realize my hands are far filthier than my clothing, my fingers black from where I've been holding the coal to write with. "I forgot all about the coal when the baby kicked. Did I smear some on my face?"

"You did," my mate agrees with a wry smile. "Let me get a cloth and you can tell me about what you are doing."

"I'm writing." I sit and wiggle in place, trying to tuck my legs under me. It's getting harder to sit compactly the more my belly grows. I kind of hope the baby will kick again, but when Ereven returns, all is quiet once more. I obediently let him clean my face with a damp, warm cloth.

"Ry-ting?" he prompts. "What is this?"

So I tell him about my plans. Well, I also have to tell him about writing and written human language, but he seems to grasp it enough that I move on to talking about the plans for the holiday—No Poison Day—and the events I'm trying to set up. "I want things to turn out well," I tell him. "So I'm writing it all out to make sure I don't forget anything. My memory's been terrible ever since I got pregnant."

"That is normal," he says, used to my complaining about that. "Maylak says it will pass."

"Which is why I'm writing," I say, and offer him my filthy hands. "Because I don't want to mess it up. I don't want to forget to include someone, or forget to do an event someone is looking forward to. Holidays are important."

"So let one of the other humans help you organize things. It sounds like a big task, and you are busy growing my son."

I snort. Busy growing a baby isn't exactly a full-time job. "I can handle it. I want to do it myself. And everyone else is busy, too. Most of the girls already have babies. They don't exactly have free time."

"Tee-fah-ni does not have a kit yet. She is pregnant, like you."

Tiff's also obsessed with trying to grow her fruit trees despite the lack of sunlight in the gorge. And when she's not busy with that, she's busy with a million other things. "She already has a ton of projects. I doubt she'll have time to hang out with me."

"What about the sisters?"

Maddie and Lila? I like them, but I don't know them as well as the others. "They're still learning how to cope with day-to-day life. I don't know that they'll have time to help either. I can do this, I promise." I clasp his hands. "I won't over-exert myself."

He thinks for a minute, then a wide smile crosses his face. "I know who can help you."

I'm starting to grow annoyed with my mate's 'helpfulness.' I don't need help with this project, but it seems he's determined to get me assistance. "Who?"

"Asha."

"Asha?" If he'd have said 'President Reagan,' I couldn't have been more surprised. Me and Asha aren't buddies. Actually, I'm not even sure we've said more than two words to each other in the last month. When Asha does emerge to spend time with the tribe, she makes a beeline for the women with babies so she can hold them. I'm not interesting to her...yet. "Why on earth would I get Asha to help me?"

"Because she needs a friend." His big hands are gentle as he places them on my belly once more. "I saw her yesterday and it made me think."

I saw her yesterday, too. "Think about what?"

"About how lonely she has been since the human females arrived." When I gesture for more information, he leans down and presses his ear to my stomach, resting his head against me in a picture of perfect contentment. "Look at things from her perspective, my mate. She has grown up desired and wanted by all the males in the tribe because there are so few females. She mates someone she is barely even friends with, and they lose their kit. Then, just when she is almost over her grieving, many new females arrive. They are all friends with each other and have their own customs. They share stories and talk and do chores together. They sit together by the fire. They are all friends. And it is something Asha has never had."

I frown to myself. I don't think anyone has been trying to deliberately exclude the prickly Asha, but now that he says it this way, I feel guilty. "What about Sevvah, Kemli and Maylak? Farli?" The tribe had females before we arrived.

"Sevvah and Kemli are both old enough to be Asha's mother. Maylak has always been Asha's rival for attention. They have never been close, and they drifted apart further when Maylak came into her healing powers and her kit lived and Asha's did not. And Farli is too young." He closes his eyes and rubs his hand on the swell of my stomach. "Do you think he will kick again?"

He's trying to distract me, I think. I poke him with my finger. "So you think I should befriend Asha?"

"I do. She could use a friend. Not just someone that is trying to hand her a child to watch. Someone that will be her friend just to be her friend."

"And you think I'm that person?"

Ereven opens his eyes and gives me another sweet smile. "Who would not want to be your friend, my Claire? You bring me such joy. I cannot imagine you doing any less for others."

He really is the dearest man. And he's got such a good heart, too. I wonder that anyone else would think about Asha's feelings, but Ereven tries to make everyone happy in his own quiet way. God, I love him. "All right, I'll go visit her and feel her out."

In the next moment, the baby moves again, and we both forget all about the holiday and Asha, focusing on the baby doing somersaults in my belly.

4

ASHA

Next Morning

I'm lying in bed, staring up at the ceiling. I don't want to go eat the morning meal with the humans today, because I can smell eggs even from here, and the thought makes my stomach hurt. I would rather not eat than eat more eggs, but Stay-see's feelings would be hurt if I turned them down. So I hide, and I contemplate the roof of the howse and watch the curls of smoke escape from our fire up to the hole at the center of the teepee.

Over in her furs, Farli's shoving on her boots and getting ready to go out, her pet dancing around her legs eagerly. I do not know why she bothers with the animal. Since we have moved to the gorge and the vee-lage, taking care of her dvisti has eaten up many of her days. Farli takes him out every day the weather is clear to graze, and just getting him out of the gorge is a time-consuming process involving a set of ropes and a thing called a pull-ee that Har-loh created. Once the creature is hauled back to the top, Farli spends her day collecting dried stalks of plants to feed him on the days when the weather is bad, and taking the bundles back to the vee-lage. Taushen goes with her and checks his traplines, but I know it is a burden. She should give up and let the stupid animal go back into the wild.

She should give up on it like Hemalo gave up on you? I do not like the thought that immediately pops into my head, and focus on something else. What should I do this day? It will be quiet since the weather is fair and warm (well, for the brutal season) and the hunters are already out, making the most of the day. Rokan says the weather will be clear for two or more days, so most of the hunters will not return home until the last moment, taking every opportunity to gather food for the tribe.

I should do the same. I should get out of my furs and see what I can help with. Stay-see loves those terrible eggs, and they are easy enough to get; I could climb and pull some nests for fuel and get more eggs for the humans. Maybe I will. Soon. But it is hard to get out of the furs when you feel there is no reason. If I do not go get eggs for Stay-see, someone else will. I do not matter, not to anyone in my tribe.

Certainly not to Hemalo.

Farli bustles out of the howse, leaving me alone with my dark thoughts. I hear her boots crunching on the fine layer of snow dusting the stones, and then her low murmur as she pauses to speak to someone. Her pet bleats, drowning out her words. Then, a moment later, she sticks her head back into the hut. "Asha, you have a visitor."

I sit up slowly, surprised. "I do?"

She nods. "I told her she could come in. I must go while the weather holds." She gives me a cheery smile and then dashes off again, letting the leather flap covering the door fall once more.

I gather my furs close to me, curious, and I am surprised when the human Claire meekly peeks inside a moment later. "Can I come in?"

"Why?" I ask.

She blinks at me with big eyes and then moves inside the howse. I notice she is carrying several large rolled-up animal hides under her arm, and she wears a bright smile on her narrow face. "I wanted your help."

I study her, trying not to scowl. I do not know Claire well. Of all the humans, she is one of the quietest of the lot, content to sit and listen when others like Jo-see would blurt all their thoughts out for all to hear. I remember that she was Bek's pleasure-mate for a time, but things soured between them, and she resonated to Ereven days after moving back to the main tribal cave. I like Ereven. It is impossible not to. But I do not know his mate well enough to say whether or not I like her. "My help?" I ask. "In what?"

Claire moves to sit next to the embers of my fire, dropping down onto Farli's favorite stool. I notice that when she moves, her thick, bundled furs make her belly look more rounded with kit than usual, and I feel a stab of jealousy and grief at the sight. I would give anything to be with kit once more, my Hashala safe in my belly.

She smooths out the hides, and I see they are covered in strange, swirly designs made of charcoal. They leak soot everywhere, and Claire grimaces as she spreads them out. "I realize this looks a little crazy, but hear me out. You heard us talking about the holiday celebration yesterday, right?"

I nod slowly, not entirely sure why this involves me. "No Poison Day. I remember."

"Yes, that's it. We're going to have another, except we're going to spread it out over several days. Well, several bad weather days." She sounds breathless and nervous, her words almost tripping over themselves in her rush to speak. It is all very curious. Why is Claire anxious about speaking to me? I am no one to her. I may be sharp to some of my tribesmates, but Claire is such a delicate, shy thing that I would not lash out at her. I fear it would break her.

"Several No Poison Days," I echo, still not sure what this has to do with me.

"Correct. I think we're going to go with eight, as a nod to Nora and Hanukkah. I think she'll like that. And it's almost kind of sort of like Epiphany or Kwanzaa, though people don't celebrate Epiphany much anymore. So I guess it's more like Kwanzaa." She stares down at the skins, thoughtful.

"Am I...supposed to know these words?"

She looks over at me, and a light flush touches her pink face. "Oh. I'm sorry. Of course not. I'm just thinking out loud." She gestures at the skins. "There's so much that I need to mentally unpack and get down on paper so I don't forget, and I feel like it's all in my head, and I don't want to forget anything. So I'm writing it out."

I frown down at the skins, then at her again. "I do not understand."

"I'm sorry. I know. I'm babbling." She clasps her hands in front of her, and somehow in the last few moments, she's managed to smear soot on her pale, flat brow. "I keep doing that. Ereven tells me to stop, too. It's just rambling and then I get away from my point and...I'm doing it again." She gives me an apologetic little smile. "Right. No Poison Day. Focus, Claire, focus."

"You wish to celebrate No Poison Day over several days," I say slowly, still trying to guess why she is involving me. "Do you... need me to show you where the local poisons are? I am not familiar with this area, but I can identify the plants if you need." I am still not sure why she would come to me instead of Kemli, who is the expert, but this is the only conclusion I can come to.

Claire blinks. "Oh, no, I don't need poison. I need help organizing things."

I am intrigued. No one ever comes to me for something like this. "You want me to help you..."

"Run the holiday celebrations, yes." She clasps her hands and puts them to her chin, her expression thoughtful. "I can try to run it all myself, but I worry I'll forget something important and mess things up. Plus, I'm not all that outgoing, and you know everyone. You can be my sa-khui ambassador."

"What about your mate?"

"He's out hunting. He won't be back until at least tomorrow, and I want to start getting the word out to people soon so they can start working on gifts."

"Farli would help you," I suggest. I think I am still in shock that someone has come to me and wants my help.

"She's busy getting food for her dvisti. And besides, Ereven told me you would be perfect to help me." Claire's smile is timid. "He said you're great at getting people to listen to you, and I'm not so good at that sort of thing."

"He suggested me?" I know Ereven well, but I had no idea he thought so highly of me. Warmth blooms in my belly. Perhaps she is right. Perhaps this is something I would be good at. Claire is definitely one of the quieter humans and could use a louder partner. "If you are certain..."

"Oh, absolutely." Her smile widens.

"Then tell me more about what you have planned." I pull my boots on and join her by the fire. I glance over at my sorry hearth. I have no food for a guest, no drinks. It has been so long that someone has come to visit that I have not given it much thought. "Do you want some tea?"

"That would be lovely."

As I throw a blend of my favorite tea flavors into my boiling pouch, Claire unravels her skins with the strange charcoal wiggles on them and tells me her plans. There will be a secret gift exchange, which sounds amusing and will allow everyone to participate and receive gifts, even if they do not have large families. After the great khui sickness, many of the tribe found themselves alone, and Claire's thoughtful suggestions about the gift game will give everyone something to look forward to.

"So you like the Secret Santa idea?" Claire asks me as I pour the tea. She looks pleased. "It's not too confusing?"

"The only confusing thing is the name," I tell her, sitting down with my own cup. It is rather nice to sit inside and talk of plans and things other than wallowing in my grief. Perhaps I have been stuck in my own head for too long. Perhaps I am just making myself miserable and need distractions. Whatever it is, Claire's presence is making me feel more like myself than I have in a long, long time. "You call it Sahn-tah?"

"Secret Santa, yes. It's because you're acting like Santa, who is the human figure that hands out gifts. He's an elf that wears red and comes down the chimney, uh, smoke hole."

I glance up at the smoke hole in my own ceiling. "It seems a strange way to deliver presents. Will they not burn?"

"It does sound weird if you pick it apart. And no, we don't have to really send our presents through smoke holes. We can leave them on people's doorsteps, or have others deliver them for us. The spirit is to have fun above all else. We can call it Secret Gifting or something else, since the Santa thing will be weird."

"I like the idea of secret gifting. It sounds fun."

Claire beams happily at my praise. "It's one of my favorite traditions, too."

We go through her list of suggestions as we drink our tea, and I help her describe them in ways that the sa-khui will remember. A day to celebrate 'Thanks-giving' becomes 'Feast Day.' An ee-stur egg hunt is changed to a seed hunt, as eggs are now a staple of our brutal season food supplies and should not be wasted on a game. The seeds of the intisar plant are big and bulbous and have a hard shell that can be painted like the small eggs Claire mentions, and then hidden around the vee-lage. It seems a silly game to me, but when she tells me it is for the kits, it makes more sense. They will enjoy such things, and the parents will enjoy watching them. There will be a day of foot-bahl and games, a day for songs and tribal gathering, and so many other plans that I find I am impressed with Claire's enthusiasm and determination to create so many things for people to do. "This is a great many tasks," I tell her. "How will you possibly keep it all straight?"

"Oh, well, the humans can read, so I thought we could post a skin with a schedule on it at the longhouse, and then maybe do pictures for the sa-khui?" She bites her lip. "It's not a great answer, but I can't think of another way to do it other than going house to house and reminding everyone what the next day will be."

"We can do both," I assure her. "I will help you." The more I think about this, the more I am determined to help Claire make this a success. It is a big task, but I am looking forward to it.

THE DAY BREEZES past as Claire and I make plans, and by the time the suns slide into the horizon and the chill in the air grows too deep to ignore, we have many more scribbles on Claire's skins, many plans, and have drunk many, many cups of tea. Claire invites me back to her small howse to eat left-over stew, and I join her. She lives in one of the small howses closer to the long-howse, where the floors are warm under the feet and the walls are decorated with strange figures. Her home is cozy but bare, much like my own, and I cannot help but think that she needs decorative skins on the walls to trap the heat and to make things pretty. I had such things in my cave back when I first mated with Hemalo, I think sadly. They were all lost in the cave-in, and I have not had the heart to decorate my new howse. Claire, I imagine, does not know how to. I can show her, if she does not mind my company. Or perhaps I will make her gifts for the exchange. I like the thought.

As we settle near the fire with our bowls, Claire stifles a yawn. "So tomorrow we go out and start talking to everyone about the Secret Gifting celebration, right?"

I nod. "It will give people time to prepare their gifts. Even small ones must be created by hand, and everyone will want to participate and make sure their tribesmate receives things they will enjoy."

She chews, nodding her head. "We can start telling people about it, hit up the hunters when they come back, and then start the celebrations at the beginning of the next moon. We'll start with Decorating Day, and then we can stagger the other days as the weather permits."

"It sounds good." I hold up my bowl. "This is good, too. Thank you for sharing."

Her smile is shy but proud. "It makes the food go further, and I don't put in too many roots because I know Ereven isn't a fan of them. And I like the company. It gets lonely when my mate is out on the trails all night."

I am absurdly pleased that she enjoys my company. I have enjoyed the day spent with Claire. She is quiet and thoughtful, unlike some of the other humans, and genuinely wants my opinions. She makes me feel...needed. Perhaps Hemalo is not the only one that has felt lost all this time. "It is good to have a friend," I tell her, and when she agrees, I think I am not the only one that feels this way. We chat quietly over the food, and then spend a bit of time sewing by the fire, until Claire's yawns become more frequent. I send her off to her furs and promise I will be back early in the morning so we can start on our plans.

When I leave her howse, I am happy. It feels strange and yet welcome to have a purpose—and a friend—again. The other humans have been friendly, of course, and my own tribesmates would perhaps not understand the difference between merely lingering by the fire next to others, and feeling truly and genuinely welcomed.

Or perhaps it has all been in my mind all this time. It is hard to say.

I return to my own little howse and find the fire is nothing but embers. Farli has not returned, and probably will not until the hunters do. Even though I complain about her company and that of her smelly pet, it feels too quiet to be here by myself. The temperature is bitingly cold, but since I am the only one in the howse, it seems a waste to make a fire for only one sa-khui. I pull a few extra furs out of my store, pile them onto my bed, and crawl under them, waiting for my body heat to warm the blankets.

As I do, I stare up at the ceiling. In the darkness, I can just make out the thick stitching on the seams, where the hides have been pulled together tightly and made to form one large covering. I think of how good I feel, how I am humming with plans and thoughts, not sadness. And I think of Hemalo and how he needs to feel needed. How I have not given that to him. How strained things are between us.

I get up out of bed, move to the wall, where the teepee top is tightly lashed down, and begin to pick the seams apart.

5

HEMALO

There is a mental calmness to working my skins. The vigorous twisting of a hard hide to make it soft, the endless rubbing of brains onto the surface, the scraping of hair. The silent weave of an awl as it guides cord through punched holes. I enjoy my task. It lets my mind settle, even when it is full of chaos. I barely notice the hour, only that the sunlight is beginning to fade. A shadow falls over my hands, making it impossible to see the tiny holes for stitches, when someone approaches and stands behind me in my leatherworking hut.

I glance up and am surprised to see Asha and the human Claire.

They stand together, Claire's strange human face wreathed in smiles. Asha wears a smile as well, but hers is warier, more cautious. It makes my heart ache to see. She is my mate. She should never be afraid to show her feelings near me. "How can

I help you?" I ask, keeping my voice level and calm, as if it is nothing to have my once-mate and a friend show up as I work.

Claire looks at Asha and then steps forward. "We wanted to talk to you about the upcoming holidays."

"Haw-lee-dehz?" I echo. "We are doing that again so soon? I thought it was for a special occasion?" I remember how Asha hated the last round of celebrations. How noisy and happy all the human females were. It seems like it was only a few turns of the moons ago.

The human looks crestfallen that I am not excited at the prospect. "Oh. Well, yes, it was not too long ago, but we thought everyone might need a little something to look forward to in order to break up the monotony of the brutal season."

She is bored? Does she think there is not enough to do? I give a wry look to the piles and piles of hides I have waiting to be worked. There has been such demand for blankets and clothing and hides for the roofs of the new howses that even my seemingly endless supply has dwindled. There are even one or two tribesmates just waiting to have a roof for their howse. There is so much to do that I cannot imagine taking the time out to play games. "If someone is bored, it is because they need to work harder."

"Oh." Claire's voice is very small. "Of course. I'm sorry we bothered you."

"Wait, Claire." Asha's arm goes around the smaller human's shoulders. She glares at me, all defiance. "This is not about you, Hemalo. You might be happy trapped in here with your piles of smelly hides, but not everyone is. This is about everyone in the tribe."

I am surprised. In the last few moons, Asha has had difficulty rousing herself to care about anything. Now she is lecturing me on tribe unity? Even though I am irritated at this sudden change, I am also fascinated at the demeanor of my mate. She is no longer listless and miserable, her eyes and her very spirit seemingly faded. Her eyes snap at me with irritation, and the hug she gives Claire is protective. There is a strength and confidence in her that I have missed seeing for a very long time.

She is beautiful, my Asha. Fiery and beautiful.

"Very well, then," I murmur. "Tell me about your haw-lee-dehz."

Asha's chin goes up, a challenging look on her face. "Are you going to listen or have you already made up your mind?"

She knows me well, my once-mate. I cannot help but smile and gesture at an open spot on the floor between spread-out skins. "You can sit and tell me about it as I work. I promise I will listen to everything you say."

"Good," Asha says, a little imperiously, and I have to bite back an even wider smile. Some of the hunters find Asha's attitude irritating, but I have always loved how strong and sure she is. I do not mind if she is thorny. Her challenging nature is one of the things I love about her, and one of the things I have missed the most.

She shepherds Claire over to the empty spot on the floor and then sits next to her. When Claire hesitates, Asha gives her an encouraging gesture, indicating that she should speak. I find this fascinating. Is it Claire that is in charge of this, or is it Asha? My fierce mate seems to have adopted Claire as a friend—startling to me, considering I have rarely seen this particular human mingle with the sa-khui. She went from Bek to Ereven and seems content to let others speak. Perhaps this is why she gets along with Asha. My mate will never let others speak for her, not if she can help it.

I feel another pang of sadness in my gut. At least, that is how the old Asha would have acted. I am not sure I even know the new Asha.

Today, however, it seems like the old Asha has returned. I continue my stitching as the two females speak. Claire's timid voice barely registers in my thoughts, though I murmur agreement to indicate I am listening. She speaks of human traditions and gift-giving and presents, but I am less interested in that than in watching my once-mate. Asha nods as Claire speaks, as if agreeing with what the human says. She occasionally adds a thought or two, and it is clear they have been hard at work thinking out this 'No Poison' celebration. It is also clear from the tension in Asha's shoulders and the stiff set of her back when our eyes meet that this is important to her.

If it is important to Asha, it is important to me. No more needs to be said. I wait for the females to pause, and then I nod slowly. "You have convinced me. What shall I do?"

Claire looks pleased, but her response is nothing compared to the triumphant look of pleasure on Asha's lovely face. I am entranced by my mate's response, and my cock—and my khui—both respond to her nearness. I feel my chest thrumming low, a rumble of pleasure at her presence. Her startled gaze meets mine, and then a scowl moves over Asha's face as I hear her khui quietly respond to mine. She does not like that I can still make her sing. Her pride is still wounded that I walked away from our mating.

Someday she will understand that I did it for her. That I finally understood that my presence was making her miserable, and I left because I could not bear to be yet another thing that caused her pain. Ask me to return, I beg silently. Tell me that you miss me in your furs. That you miss the warmth of our bodies together. Tell me that you miss my smile like I miss yours. All will be forgotten in an instant and we can be back together tonight. Now. In the next moment.

But Asha only lifts her chin, her eyes narrowing at me. She hears my song and she does not like it.

She needs more time. Very well.

"Wonderful," Claire says, oblivious to the tension simmering between myself and Asha. "We're going to start the calendar of events on the first bad weather day of the next moon-turn." She pulls out a skin and unrolls it, then gets out a piece of charcoal. "I'm going to record who you get for your secret gift partner, and you'll need to make that person a series of small gifts and trinkets to be given out every celebration day. We have eight of them, so you'll need to make eight gifts."

I nod in understanding, my gaze locked with Asha's combative one. "And what if I wish to give someone else a gift?"

"It is not allowed," Asha replies sharply. "You are to give gifts to your secret partner."

"Oh, actually, that's quite fine," Claire says in a timid voice, and earns a quick frown from Asha. "I mean, the holidays are all about giving and lifting each other up. It's perfectly fine to give as many gifts as you choose. You just need to make sure that you do the eight small gifts for the secret exchange to be fair to the person you are assigned. Think of it like a game. The eight gifts are part of the rules. Anything you do outside is your own business, of course."

My mate does not look as if she enjoys being contradicted by mild Claire, but she eventually shrugs. "Give gifts to whoever you want. I care not."

"Is that so?" I say, deliberately baiting her. No one has ever accused Asha of caring too little. She is a hot flame of emotion, my mate, and burns hottest in an argument. Her scowls please me, though. An irritated Asha is a welcome sight after her sadness for so long. I will take her venom happily.

"Just be careful you do not overburden yourself with your gift-giving, Hemalo," Claire advises me, making lines on the rolled-up hide with the charcoal. At any other time, I might be interested in what she is doing. Today, with Asha seated in front of me, so fierce and so achingly like her old self that it makes my heart beat fast—and ache with need at the same time—I cannot concentrate on anything but my mate. Claire continues, oblivious. "Can you have him draw and let me know what he picks?"

Asha gives me another defiant look. She pulls out a small pouch she has at her belt and opens it up, then holds it out to me. "Pick one strip and give it to me."

Interesting. I decide not to prick at her any longer and obediently reach into the pouch. I pull out a small strip of worn leather that has more of the strange charcoal lines on it and hold it out to Asha.

"Here, Claire," Asha says, giving her the slip. "What does it say?"

Claire looks up and peers at the scrap, then nods. "Maylak is your secret partner."

I grunt. I have known Maylak ever since she was a small kit, and it is easy to think of things to give her: a new pouch for her favorite tea, hoods and boots for her kits, a new blanket for her to share with her mate, soft leather so she can create a new tunic for herself... "I am pleased."

"Hmph." Asha does not look happy. "That is too easy. He should draw a different name. Claire, make him draw again."

"Oh, but I don't think..." Claire purses her lips. "Is there a problem with it being Maylak?"

"Yes," Asha says at the same time that I say "No."

I am surprised at Asha's displeasure. "I like Maylak very much," I say. "I can make her some very lovely gifts."

Asha just makes a harrumphing noise and crosses her arms. Claire looks uneasy, as if she has stepped into something unpleasant.

"Do not worry," I cannot help but tease. "I will make you something far more spectacular, Asha."

"Do not bother," she says in a tart voice, though I can tell my suggestion has pleased her. "Make your silly gifts for the healer. I need nothing from you."

"That sounds like a challenge," I reply. "Are you sure you need nothing?" Her nostrils flare, and she licks her lips, her tongue darting between sharp teeth. My cock aches again. When she doesn't respond, I continue. "Perhaps I will think of something to give you that you might want."

"From you? There is nothing." Her voice is lofty and arrogant, and she unfolds her long legs, getting to her feet in a graceful, fluid motion to rival any hunter's. "You gave up on me, and I do not care what you do. Come, Claire. Let us go see if Shorshie is busy."

"Oh, okay." Claire looks at me and then back at Asha as she sashays out of the hut, her tail flicking with irritation. Mystified, the little human gathers her things, gives me a distracted smile, and then hurries after her friend.

I smile to myself, my leatherwork forgotten as I watch the two females leave. Asha's barbs were meant to scratch, but I do not mind. She was vibrant today, vibrant and alive and full of the bright spirit I remember. It makes my heart glad. I gaze down at the leather in my lap and then cast it aside. If I will be making gifts for Maylak, I will make even better ones for my Asha. She has long been a rival of the healer, and I need to make her realize there is no reason to be jealous.

There has only ever been one female in my eyes.

6

CLAIRE

One Week Later

"Welcome home," I tell my mate as he pushes aside the privacy flap over the doorway and saunters in, shedding layers of clothing as he comes in. I love my Ereven, but he's a bit of a slob. It's like there's too much going on in his head for him to hold it all in, and it pours out in small ways, like the fact that his hair always seems to be slightly tangled, or the piles of clothing he leaves wherever he drops them. I don't mind it, though—I'm just glad he's home. It's been three long days and nights without him. "Storm starting up?"

He pulls me close before I can pluck the clothes off the floor and gives me an enthusiastic kiss. He smells like sweat, and his clothes are damp with ice, but oh, his kiss is distracting. "I missed you, my mate," he murmurs as he presses a few more kisses to my mouth. “Each night away seems to be longer than the last.”

“Then you will be pleased to hear that Rokan came back to Croatoan a few hours ahead of you and said the weather would be bad for the next two days.”

His eyes light up. “That is good. That means I get to spend time in the furs with my mate.”

I can feel a blush creeping over my cheeks. “You can.”

He presses another kiss to my forehead and then sheds another layer of furs. The ends of his hair have iced over, and there’s a slick layer of ice on his horns. “I look forward to a day of terrible stew and equally terrible eggs. Tell me you have something for your poor starving mate to eat?”

I giggle, because my ‘poor starving mate’ is a picky eater. He loves raw meat and raw meat and that’s about it. He’ll eat other things, but he likes to joke about how terrible they are. “Stew?”

Ereven clutches his belly, grinning. “I can hardly wait to choke it down.”

I laugh, moving toward the fire as he continues to strip off clothing. “How was your hunting? You were gone a long time, so I hope it went well?”

“Very well,” he says, stripping off his tunic. “I filled one cache again and brought a pair of fat dvisti down into the gorge. They’re in one of the storage huts until I can butcher them.”

“Yum,” I tease. Dvisti is my least favorite of the meats we eat, mostly because they remind me of shaggy, ugly ponies. But I’ll eat it. I’m just happy that the hunting has been so great lately. The pinched, worried look has eased from the faces of the hunters, and even Vektal looks like he’s finally slept a full night recently. I'll eat pony if I have to. The baby growing in my belly needs food, and I'm not going to be picky. "I'm glad the hunting went well," I tell Ereven. "One less thing for everyone to worry about." Even my easy-going mate has expressed concerns about the food situation, but it sounds like that'll be in the past soon enough.

"Very well. Now feed me, female, before I am overcome by my mate's beauty and tackle her to the furs."

I choke back a laugh at that, moving toward the fire where I have the last of the stew warming in the pouch. His mate hasn't felt particularly beautiful lately, what with my belly growing by leaps and bounds and my ankles seeming to swell to keep pace with it. I've felt fat and bloated for days, and I have almost another year of being pregnant ahead of me—joy. I ladle the stew into one of the bowls and hand it over to Ereven.

He immediately grabs me by the hips and pulls me into his lap, ignoring the bowl. He nuzzles at my neck instead. "Too late. I am overcome."

"You should eat," I chide him, squirming. I love the way he fusses over me, always making me feel beautiful.

"Why should I? There is something much more pleasant to put my mouth on."

"You'll...need your strength."

"Ah." He presses one last smacking kiss on my mouth and then takes the bowl. "Always wise, my Claire." He takes an enthusiastic bite of stew, grimaces, and then shoves another mouthful in. "Tell me what you have been up to," he says between bites. "How go the No Poison Day plans?"

"Fantastic." I put an arm around his neck, making myself comfortable in his lap as he eats. "We've got everyone signed up for the secret gift exchange, and there's a lot of excitement. Nora told Dagesh about the Jewish tradition of dreidels, and now he's making one for each kit in the tribe." I think it's the sweetest, and it goes to show just how thoughtful Nora's mate is. "And then there's decorating, which is first on the celebration days. We lost our decorations from the last holiday, but Farli said she saw a few of the rekrek bushes that are good for stringing seeds, so she promised to get some of those for next time. And Liz said she and Raahosh will get us a tree."

"And presents?" he asks, scooping another bite of stew into his mouth. "We still have time to work on those, yes? I have not finished Borran's decorated waterskins yet."

"Plenty of time," I assure him. The moons don't turn for another week and some change, though everyone's already eagerly looking forward to the beginning of the celebrations.

"What happens if someone gives a gift early?"

"Oh, well, I suppose that's all right, though it's not much in the spirit of the game."

"Did you decide to play, after all?"

I tilt my head at him, curious. "Of course not. I'm running things. Someone has to make sure things go smoothly. Why do you ask?"

He shrugs and sets his empty bowl aside. "Because there is a wrapped package next to the door."

"What?" I pry out of his arms and stagger to my feet. "There is?"

"Shall I get it?" He gets up as well.

"No, I've got it." I head to the door and push back the flap, peering out. Sure enough, there is a small, fur-wrapped package on the step. Curious, I pick it up and look around. "Did you see who left this?"

"It was there when I arrived. Perhaps someone is playing early?"

Or they don't understand the rules. It makes me sad, because both Asha and I have worked so hard to get everyone to pay attention. I know we're throwing a lot at them, but it's all in fun, and everyone seemed to understand the concepts when asked. "Perhaps it's for you?" Except Georgie is his secret gift partner, and I'm pretty sure she grasps the rules, being human and all. There's no cultural misunderstanding there.

"Open it and see?"

I offer it to my mate, but he shakes his head. After a moment's hesitation, I pull the sinew-cord tie off of the small square package and unwrap it. It's mostly hide, but in the center is a delicate, shining bone bracelet. It's been worked with care and precision, the carving delicate and beautiful, and someone's spent hours on this to make it glossy and lovely to wear.

"That is not for me," Ereven says with a grin. "I do not think it would fit over my hand."

He's right. The size is definitely human. It's so pretty, and yet... I'm not playing the game. I shouldn't be getting any gifts. "I'll have to talk to Asha in the morning and see if she can think who would have left this."

"Until then," my mate says, and puts his arms around my waist, "you are all mine."

7

ASHA

Two Weeks Later
Decorating Day

"And you don't have any idea?" The look on Claire's face is frustrated. "I've gotten three gifts now. We haven't even started playing until today."

I shake my head, putting the final stitches on a soft little tunic, perfect for a kit. It is dyed a dark reddish color with light, contrasting stitches, and while I am not the best at sewing, I am pleased with it and its contrasting sister tunic made of buff leather with dark stitches. No-rah's secret gift-giver is Warrek, and he has not been himself since his father passed, so I am helping him along. "Perhaps someone simply wishes to give you gifts?"

"But who?" Claire puts down the colored seeds she is stringing. "We've checked and everyone says they know the rules. You know I'm not playing."

I shrug. I am not nearly as concerned as my friend. "Take the gifts and be thankful. It is a kind gesture."

This is not a good enough answer for Claire. In the days we have been spending together, I have learned that she is quiet, but when she plants her feet, she is more stubborn than an old dvisti. I can tell by the look on her face that she will not rest until she solves this. "I just want to know who and understand why."

"It is as you have said—it is the awful-day spirit."

"Holiday spirit," she corrects.

"Same thing," I tease. "Your human words all sound the same."

She gives a little irritated snort, and I bite back a grin. Spending time with Claire is fun. Just having a friend to talk to makes even the most monotonous of chores entertaining, and I see now why the human females are so quick to cluster together on a daily basis and share stories. Having a friend your own age is...vastly enjoyable. I have never felt friendly with Maylak, and I do wonder if that is my own fault. I have always seen her as competition, never as a friend. She was always so perfect, so lovely, so talented with her healing, that I felt I had to be that much more flirty with all the males of the tribe to get any attention. There is no competing with Claire, just friendship.

It is...nice.

Claire glances over at the little tunics I am finishing, and a true smile returns to her face. "Those are so cute. Nora will love them."

"Warrek has done a wonderful job," I agree slyly. "He is a good gift-giver."

"And you are sweet to help him," Claire says with a squeeze on my arm. We both know he has been sucked into the blackness of despair since his father died. I know this feeling all too well, and it makes me feel good to help out. He will be himself again soon enough. Until then, I will assist how I can.

"I am done for now," I tell her, knotting the last stitch and then biting the cord. "Shall we go see how the decorations are coming?"

"Probably a good idea. Let me finish these seeds and we can check on Josie." She strings a little faster, and I fold up and hide the tiny tunics under a basket of dried tea leaves. Once Claire is done, we take the string and put on our wraps, heading to the center of the vee-lage. The weather is terrible, and Claire shivers and makes chattering noises the moment we step outside. I carry the strings of seeds so she can tuck her hands into her clothing, but it is cold even for me. There is a thin layer of ice on the stones, which makes them slippery, and we take our time picking our way across the vee-lage toward the long-howse. The air is frosty cold, and the wind howls above, snowflakes drifting down despite the protective lip of the gorge. From a distance, I can see the tall, thin stalk of the decorating tree sticking out from the roof of the long-howse. As we get closer, I can hear the excited chatter of people. Everyone is enjoying Claire's No Poison celebrations, and I am proud of my friend for setting this all up. She has a good heart.

"I can hear Josie," she muses as we approach the long-howse.

"It is impossible not to," I retort. Jo-see is the most chattery of the humans, with a mouth that never stops moving and a high-pitched voice that seems to cut through the air. How her surly mate tolerates all that talking, I do not know, but Haeden seems blissfully content. Thinking of them and their happiness makes me think of my once-mate, Hemalo. I have not seen him in the last few days, and a pang of loneliness hits me. Is he enjoying the celebration? Is he pleased at making gifts for the healer? I hate that I care. I should not. He has abandoned me.

And yet I cannot stop my thoughts from turning to him, time and time again.

We enter the long-howse, and people are everywhere, laughing and talking. The tree that has been selected for decorating rests in a large basket, soil tucked around the bulbous root. It will be eaten on Feast Day, and until then, the tree will be laden with garlands and ornaments and colorful fluttering disks made of hard leather or papery tree bark. Jo-see is near the center of it all, holding little Esha up so she can adjust a string of colorful seeds on one of the thin, wobbly branches. Clumps of poison plants have been hung from the ceiling, and underneath one, Mah-dee kisses her mate with enthusiasm. More poison leaves are strung up on sinew cords, fluttering as they are hung from the rafters. Nearby, others in the tribe make garlands and laugh together, and several of the hunters are stringing even more garlands around the lodge and Tee-fa-ni's potted plants. Everyone seems to be enjoying themselves. I do not see the appeal, and I think the tree looks terrible with so many things piled atop it, but humans have strange traditions that make them happy, so I go along with it.

Claire claps her mittens together happily at the sight of the ugly tree covered in even uglier decorations. "It looks so great!"

"Doesn't it?" Leezh comes up beside us, tossing her yellow mane. "I feel like Cindy Lou Who in the center of Whoville post-Grinch!"

"What?" I blink at the humans.

"Nothing," Claire says with a laugh. She hugs my arm. "Just Liz saying crazy things like usual."

Leezh does tend to say strange things. "Where is your mate?" I ask Claire. "Shall we find him?"

She searches the busy groups, and then points off into the corner. "There, hanging garlands with Lila and Rokan." She lights up at the sight of him and looks over at me. "Should we give him our garland while they're busy?"

I wordlessly hand it over to her, biting back my smile. Claire is a good friend, but she is still in the early days of her mating and is always pulled away by the thought of her mate. I do not mind this. I was like this once, I think.

Then I frown to myself. All of my memories of Hemalo and I in a cave together are unpleasant ones, of me sniping at him or making angry comments. Of him trying to please me and me pushing away his help. Maybe I was never like that, after all. Perhaps I was never a good mate. I feel sad at the thought. Perhaps it is good that Hashala never got to see her parents like this. A mating should be for life, and I drove my mate away with my bitterness.

I watch Claire cross the long-howse with the garland. Leezh sidles up next to me, a curious look in her eyes. "So where is your mate, Asha?"

I scowl at her. "He left me. You know this."

She shrugs, unruffled by my angry tone. "All I know is that you're looking at Claire and Ereven like they're cake and you're on a diet. And I'm thinking maybe you're working too hard to convince yourself that you hate Hemalo."

"You think I hate him? He abandoned me."

"You pushed him away." She lifts her shoulders again in another small, careless shrug. "I'm not going to say being mated to Raahosh is nothing but daisies and kittens. Sometimes you have to make a relationship work. And I'm just saying maybe you should have tried a little harder. He lost his kit, too, you know."

Anger burns in my gut, and I am filled with the sudden urge to scratch her smirking human eyes out. But Leezh is carrying a child in her belly, and her mate stands nearby holding their small daughter and talking to the chief and his mate. She is bold with her words, but she is needed by them. And I somehow feel that if I defended myself...no one would take my side. They would just shake their heads at sad, angry Asha.

This day is ruined for me. "You do not know of what you speak, Leezh."

"Then tell me," she says in a soft voice. "Help me understand and maybe I can help you, too. I'm not trying to be a bitch, Asha. I just see you unhappy and I want to help."

"I do not want your help," I snap at her, and turn on my foot, leaving behind the happy celebration. Let the others celebrate No Poison Day. I am retreating to my howse, where it is quiet and safe and no one will bother me.

I storm across the vee-lage, but once I leave the long-howse, it is quiet. Everyone is gathered there, enjoying the day. I am happy for Claire that things are going so well, but I no longer want to be part of it. I just want to hide again. I want my blankets and I want to not think about the once-mate that I have hurt or the kit I have lost. I do not want to think about anything right now.

Leezh can sympathize with Hemalo, but I cannot forget that he abandoned me. He left me. I needed him and he gave up on me. Thinking of him hurts, and I am so tired of feeling as if I am the one constantly in the wrong. Why does no one see that I am in pain, too? That just because I do not cry prettily like the humans or give everyone sad eyes, I am not walking with an open wound in my chest where my heart should be? Why can I not wear my pain differently? But no, because Hemalo has left me alone, I am somehow the flawed one. I am the problem.

I swipe aside the privacy flap to my howse and storm inside. Because my thoughts are full of Hemalo, it is somehow unsurprising to see him there inside. His back is to me, and he stands over my furs, gazing up at the teepee ceiling. His hands are on his hips, and his tail flicks in that restless, constant way of his. I suddenly remember lying in bed with him, laughing because his tail flicks so much, and so often I would tease him that I would never be able to sleep.

But that was a very different time from now. We had good times between the arguments, once. Now there is nothing left but a void.

Still, I cannot help but be secretly pleased to see him here. Has he come to visit me? To tell me that he loves me and misses me? That he is sorry for abandoning me? "What are you doing here?" The words sound abrasive and cold the moment they leave my mouth.

He turns slowly to look at me, his movements a leisurely contrast to that endless flicking of his tail. "Farli told me you had a tear in your roof. I came to look at it." His voice is liquid and deep, and the sound of it fills me with longing. Hemalo is a handsome male, and his body is big and strong. But his voice, oh, his voice is something special. Just hearing it makes my khui react, and it gives a low, pleasurable hum.

"So you are only here because Farli asked you?"

He turns back to the walls of the howse and examines it closer. "Why else would I be here? You certainly would not invite me."

That hurts. I have been thinking about him, a lot. It is just... hard to unbend and admit that he has hurt me with his leaving. That I wish for him to give me a second chance. That I am the one that is the problem. The very thought stings my pride. "Why should I invite you?" I snap back. "You have made it quite clear how you feel."

Hemalo gives me a focused, intense look, and then turns back to the roof. He fingers the covering and the torn stitches that bind two of the hides together. "You should invite me so the snow does not fall on you as you sleep. Or do you like waking up covered in meltwater?"

I shrug, feeling defensive. "It will get repaired soon enough." I do not tell him that I picked apart the stitches to invite him over for such a meeting, but my courage failed me and I did not follow through. Curse Farli and her interfering. I am not ready to talk to Hemalo. I hate it when he judges me, when he gives me those knowing looks that make me feel foolish. When he treats me like I am a kit.

"It will never get repaired if you do not let me know there is a problem." There is a rebuke in his mild tone, even as he examines the thick stitching. Then he holds an end out and gazes over at me. "Was this cut?"

"What? Do not speak of ridiculous things."

The look he shoots me is thoughtful. "If this tore, it would not tear in such a neat fashion."

"Why would I cut it?" I snarl at him, jerking his hand away from the cords as if they will somehow accuse me, too.

"I do not know. That is why I am asking." He grabs my hand before I can pull back, and then his fingers lock with mine. "You are angry, Asha." His voice is a low whisper. "Why are you so angry?"

My heart speeds up at his nearness, my khui reacting to his presence. It is only that I have not mated in such a long time, I tell myself. That is why the brush of his skin against mine makes every muscle in my body tense. That is why my tail begins to flick so rapidly against my leg, and my cunt gets wet with need. It is only because I miss mating. It is not because I miss Hemalo. "I am not angry," I protest.

A slow smile curls his mouth. "You think I do not know you? That I do not know your moods?" His thumb strokes over my knuckles. "Are you angry because Farli asked me to fix the roof, or are you angry because it is me here and everything I do makes you angry?"

Does he truly think that? That everything he does makes me upset? I jerk my hand from his, because I feel as if I am being accused all over again. "I said I was not angry. Though now I am getting irritated that you think I do not speak the truth about that."

He sighs heavily, watching me. "No matter what I say, it ends in a fight with you, does it not?"

"Why do you think I wish to fight? Why are you always trying to make me feel like the bad one in a fight? Like I am doing something wrong?"

Hemalo shakes his head at me, his mane flicking. "That is not what I meant at all." He puts a big hand to his forehead and rubs the base of his horns, like he always does when he has a headache. "I am doing this all wrong. My apologies. I did not come here to make you upset."

"Then why are you here?"

"I came to help."

Instead of making me feel better, his words just make my khui hum faster, and my cunt aches with need. I press my thighs tightly together and cross my arms over my chest. My teats tingle with awareness at his nearness, but I try to ignore that. Now is not the time. "You should be with the tribe," I tell him, and gesture in the direction of the long-howse. "Celebrating."

He shrugs and turns back to the roof, eyeing the hole I have created (and denied). "I do not feel like there is much to celebrate." His hand caresses the leather.

I am startled to hear him say that. Hemalo has always had such an even, calm personality, unlike my fiery temper. It sounds like something that would come from my mouth, not his. "The humans, especially Claire, have been working very hard to make this enjoyable for the entire tribe," I chastise him.

"You have been working alongside them," he reminds me. Hemalo glances over his shoulder at me, and it nearly takes my breath away. My tail patters against my leg with excitement, coiling and flicking. "I am glad they have finally accepted you."

Accepted me?

His words sting. Saying they 'accept' me makes it sound as if I am the outsider. This is my tribe. I was here first. And it hurts my feelings. "Spare me your pity," I tell him. "If I wanted to hear what you thought, I would have asked you to come to the howse. There is a reason why it was Farli that asked you here, not me."

I hate the words even as they spit forth from my mouth like daggers. They are needles designed to launch and hurt, and they succeed. I can see the look on his face as his expression changes, growing cold. It is as if the warmth in his eyes ices over and leaves nothing but frost. Just like that, we are enemies again. My body needs his, but our spirits will never understand one another.

"I am sorry I came," Hemalo says. Even now, his voice is so beautiful and pleasant that I want to weep. "Tell Farli I will be back to fix it tomorrow." He steps away from the hole in the roof, and then moves carefully away from me, where I stand hugging my chest and hating the anger that fills me. "I will make sure to come by when you are not home."

And now I am the one being hurt. This is what I want, right? But the thought of him deliberately avoiding me, deliberately avoiding my howse when I am here because he does not wish to talk to me? Even as it makes me angry, it also hurts and makes me feel empty inside. But I lift my chin. "Good. Leave. It is what you are best at."

He stiffens. Hemalo stops and turns back to me. His nostrils flare and his tail flips wildly, the only signs that I have upset him. "You say that as if you think I wanted to leave."

"Did you not?"

"No." The quiet word echoes in the howse between us.

My heart flutters wildly. "If it was something you did not wish to do," I say, stepping forward, my every movement a confrontation, "it seemed rather easy for you to do."

"Is that what you think?" He takes a step toward me, and I realize he is devouring me with his eyes, his khui humming. "That it is easy for me to walk away?"

"Should I think differently?" I whisper. I can barely hear my own thoughts over the pounding of my heart. Why am I so nervous around him? So very tense? It is like my entire body is coiled into one anxious knot.

Hemalo gazes down at me, and I think for a moment that he is going to touch me. That he will reach out and brush his knuckles over my cheek. Just the thought of that small touch makes my body react, and my khui hums even louder. His joins it, and the song between us seems to fill the air.

It takes me a moment to realize what is happening. That the joined song of our khuis should not be so loud, so overwhelmingly strong that they take over the air around us. That my pulse should not be thrumming so hard that my heart feels as if it will leap from my chest. That I should not be so very aroused by the nearness of my mate.

I open my mouth, and the humming of my khui is so loud it erupts from my throat, my entire body vibrating with the ferocity of its song.

Resonance.

Hemalo's eyes widen in surprise. His hand goes to his chest and he places his palm flat over the center of his heart, as if he can feel the heart beating under the plating there. I can hear it, though. I can hear his khui singing to mine.

"Resonance," he breathes, speaking the word aloud.

We are to mate again. We are to mate and have another kit.

I am...terrified. Completely and utterly terrified.

8

HEMALO

The wonder of the moment disappears in a heartbeat.

Resonance. I am to have a kit again. I am to bond with my mate again. Joy bursts through me, like the suns coming through the clouds after a long snowstorm. Even as I feel the smile spreading across my face, Asha begins to tremble. Her face pales, until she is so pale blue that she is almost the color of one of the strange-looking humans. Her tail goes limp. "No," she breathes.

No?

This is the best thing that has ever happened to me. I am filled with joy at the thought of being able to experience the wonder of resonance with the female I love—again. To bring another kit into this world. To get a second chance with everything.

And my heart feels as if it is being squeezed by a fist when her eyes well up and she begins to cry.

She does not want this. She does not want a second chance. "Do not cry, Asha. Please." I begin to panic, my mind spinning through possible things to say to calm her tears. "Nothing has to be done."

She gives me an incredulous look. "Nothing has to be done? We have resonated! There is no denying resonance!"

"Yet," I say. "Nothing has to be decided yet." I will give her as much time as my body will physically allow me. It does not matter if resonance makes me deathly ill—I will not push Asha into something that will hurt her spirit.

She throws her hands in the air. "Why do I even speak to you?"

Because you have no choice? I want to say, but she is already panicking. "Is resonating to me again so awful?" I know I have never been her mate of choice, but surely she would grow used to the idea over time? It is not inconceivable to resonate a second time to a mate, or even three or four times. But Asha acts staggered, as if I have plunged a knife into her chest.

She shakes her head slowly. "I...I cannot. Hemalo, I cannot." She moves forward, and I think she moves to hug me, but her hands grip my vest, and the panic in her face is overwhelming to see.

"Do you not wish another kit?"

Agony moves over her face. "I...I do not know. I want Hashala. That is who I want."

My poor mate. "She is gone," I say gently, covering her hands with mine. "We cannot bring her back with thoughts or hopes. If so, she would be in your arms even now." I reach out and caress her cheek. "But we can try again. We can have another kit. Resonance wants us to have another kit. And perhaps this time, we will have a healthy one to love and take care of."

Asha moves away from me as if burned. "I *love* her," she spits at me, suddenly furious. "She may have only lived for a hand of hours, but I loved her so. I still do."

"I do, too. Do you think the pain of grief is solely yours?"

Her shaking hands press to her mouth. "I am so scared, Hemalo."

I know she is. I know exactly what she is thinking. She is not scared of being mated to me—she is scared of it all going wrong again. Of the tentative, fragile bond we had between us being destroyed once more in the wake of unending grief. Of loss. Of bringing something so small, so fragile, and so loved into this world only to have it taken from you as quickly as it arrived. She does not need to say any of this. I know. Oh, I know.

I want this kit.

I want my mate, and I want my kit. I want the same happiness that the others in the tribe have. I think once Asha's head clears, she will realize this is a wonderful thing. That we cannot live in fear or grief, but must keep living and loving. She will realize that Hashala would have wanted a sister or a brother. She would want her parents to be happy. "It is a good thing," I tell her, and reach out to touch her again.

She pushes away from me, a panicked look on her face, and I realize I am going about this all wrong.

Asha needs time. I realize, slowly, even as my body throbs and aches with need for her, that I must give her time. The more I push and prod at her for something, the more she wants to run away. She does not like to be forced into something—one reason why our resonance went so sour. She likes for things to be her decision. She is stubborn, my mate. Stubborn and magnificent.

She will come to terms with our resonance, but she must come to it in her own time.

My presence at her side will be seen as pushing her. Not to the tribe, who thinks we should be together, but to Asha, who resents that she did not choose me. I suspect she has always felt a bit trapped with me as her mate. I am not a hunter, nor am I the handsomest or cleverest in the tribe. I am steady when she craves excitement.

I am also patient, though. I know how Asha's mind works. The more I push her to accept this, the harder she will fight. This is why I could not help her when she was grieving. This is why I had to leave our mating.

She does not want me at her side. Until she comes to me and says she wishes to have me in her furs, I must give her space. The thought makes me ache, and I hate that it must be so. Why can I not take my mate in my arms and hug her? Rub noses and twine my tail with hers? Why must everything between us be a fight?

It makes me tired.

So I take her trembling hand in mine and give it a squeeze. "Asha," I say, my voice low and calm. I must act as if I am not affected, as if her presence is not driving me wild with need. "Nothing must be done right away. I will leave and give you time to think about things."

"What is there to think about?" she asks, and there is a bitter note in her voice. "It has already been decided. I am to be a mother even if my body cannot hold a kit and my mate hates me."

"I do not hate you." Hate is the furthest thing I feel for her. But I know that trying to hold Asha is like trying to hold a handful of snow—the tighter I grip, the more she will trickle between my fingers and disappear. "Rest," I tell her. "Relax. We will talk in the morning."

My slow, even words seem to finally get through to her. She nods, her movements jerky. "I need time to think."

"I know." I give her hand one final squeeze. "Take all the time you need."

And because I love her, I will not be here when she finally comes to seek me.

CLAIRE

Song Day

"No, not another!" I moan in protest as one of the carolers approaches me with a gift. "I'm not playing!"

"Just take it and enjoy it," Farli says with a toss of her hair. She is practically dancing with excitement at the fact that I'm getting an unexpected gift.

It's day two of the celebrations, and the tribe—both sa-khui and human—have thrown themselves into the festivities with an enthusiasm that makes my heart glad. The longhouse has been decorated to the nines, and every inch of the place flutters with homemade seed-or-bark garlands, and our spindly, sad, pink tree is potted and sticks out of the opening in the roof of the lodge itself, too weak and unsteady to support a star or an angel topper. It doesn't matter. Decorating Day was a success and everyone enjoyed it. The first of the Secret Santa—excuse me,

Secret *Gifting*—gifts were handed out, and I've seen people showing off new gloves, scarves, and sharing treats from their gift-givers. It's been fun to watch the excitement, and no one seems to mind when one particularly un-sneaky gift-giver or two gets caught in the act. It all adds to the merriment.

Today is the second day of terrible weather, which means we are plowing ahead with the next day of festivities—Song Day. It's a mix of Christmas caroling and summer camp, as we are all hanging around by the blazing fire, roasting food on skewers and singing whatever songs come to mind. The sa-khui are terrible, tone-deaf singers and don't have many songs that aren't completely made up on the spot, so most of the actual singing falls back to the humans. It's all fun, though. Everyone loved it when Tiffany sang 'Ave Maria' (perfectly, of course, because Tiffany is flawless) and they are currently enjoying Liz's Batman version of 'Jingle Bells.' She and Josie are playing a game of one-up on who can think of the most annoying song, because between the two of them we've heard 'John Jacob Jingleheimer Schmidt' and 'Henry the Eighth' and 'This is the Song that Never Ends,' which the sa-khui found utterly hilarious. I'm having fun...or at least I was until the newest present showed up.

This is gift number four. Gift number two was a pouch of tea, and gift number three, a carved comb for my hair. I take the gift from Farli and hold it up, showing Ereven from across the fire where he sits next to Vektal and Georgie. He just shakes his head and laughs, amused at my frustration.

For a bit, I thought that Ereven was sneakily being the one providing gifts, but he's been too surprised with each reveal, and it made me realize pretty quickly that it's not him. It's someone else, and no one's coming forward. But who, and why? Frustrated, I pull open the tie on the pouch, acutely aware of the fact that a dozen people are watching me with interest. It's a small tribe, and the gossip will be all over every hut before the hour is over. I peer inside, and the smell of toffee hits me. "Hraku seeds," I announce. "Whoever it is, thank you."

"Share the wealth," Josie announces, making grabby hands at me.

I gladly hand them over to her. Josie's having pregnancy cravings like mad and loves sweets. Stacy's been trying to keep her supplied with things to munch on, but Josie's been hoovering them up faster than Stacy can cook. "They're all yours."

"Oh, but it's your gift. I only want a few." She hesitates.

"I'm sure my gift-giver won't mind me sharing with the tribe," I say with a big smile, acting pleased that I've received another gift. In truth, it bugs me. I don't like feeling beholden to anyone, and the fact that I'm getting all these gifts makes me worry what I'm overlooking. I'm afraid I'm going to turn around one day and someone will be there with their hand outstretched, expecting a favor or a gift of their own in return.

"I'll get my skillet," Stacy says with a grin, getting up from her seat by the fire next to her mate and child. "I suppose if we're having a bonfire, we should have the Not-Hoth version of s'mores, too."

Josie squeals with excitement. "Yay!"

"Who sings next?" someone asks.

"I will," Megan says, standing up. She clears her throat dramatically and puts a hand out in front of her like an opera singer. "Me me me me me," she sings, warming up. People giggle at her theatrics.

Her mate Cashol nods. "It is a simple song, but I like it. The words are easy to remember."

"That's not the song, babe." She winks at him and then begins to sing the Hokey Pokey, complete with movements. A few people groan, but Esha and Sessah love it, moving along with Megan as she sings.

Stacy returns by the end of the song, and Georgie gets to her feet. "I just want to say how great the celebrations have been so far, and we have Claire to thank for it." She claps her hands, and then everyone is clapping for me. It's a gesture the sa-khui aren't too familiar with, judging by the awkward smacks of their hands together, but the smiles and nods are universal.

"It's nothing, really," I say, feeling shy. "And Asha's been such a big help." I look around the fire for her, but she still hasn't joined the group. Huh. I went to her house this morning, but Farli said she was sleeping in and she'd be along shortly. It's been hours. Now I feel like the worst friend ever because I've been having fun and didn't notice that she was missing. Is something wrong, I wonder? I look for her ex, but I don't see Hemalo either.

And now I begin to worry. That's not a good sign. I worry they've argued and Asha's fragile happiness has disappeared again.

I get up and murmur something about heading to the ladies' room, patting my belly as an excuse, and then head out into the village, making a beeline for Asha's little house. There's no smoke curl coming out of the teepee roof—no surprise given that everyone's at the bonfire today—but it's also super cold, which makes me worry about her. If I feel like my breath is crystallizing into ice in my lungs away from the warmth of the fire, it can't feel much better for her. It's more than that, though.

She's my friend, and I hate the thought of her being miserable when everyone else is having so much joy right now.

The privacy flap is over the door of the hut, and I hesitate, sa-khui etiquette ingrained in my brain. It's the height of rudeness to speak to someone through the thing, but at the same time... she might need a friend. I drag my fingers over the edge of the flap, scratching at it in the alien way of 'knocking.' "Hello?" I call softly. "Asha, are you in there? It's me, Claire."

There's a noise from within, but it doesn't quite sound like a "come in." I decide I'm going to interpret it as just that and claim poor human hearing if she gets upset. I push my way inside and glance around.

Asha's here, all right. It's bitterly cold inside, and the room is dark. She's not sleeping, though. She's seated in her furs, staring up at the roof, where a large gap has broken in the stitching of the hides that make up the teepee.

"Did that just happen?" I ask, moving to stand near her bedding. "Should I go get someone?"

"It has been that way for days," Asha says in a curiously mild voice, almost as if she is half-asleep. "It is fine."

Is it? I eye the hole and then look down at her. She doesn't look upset, but has a thoughtful expression on her face. Her hair is braided and smooth, and she's wearing her favorite tunic, which tells me that she hasn't just woken up. "Are you feeling all right?"

She nods after a moment and then glances over at me.

"Can I sit?"

"Of course." She moves over a little and pats the furs.

It's no easy task to get my increasingly ungainly body down on the floor and into the pile of furs, but I manage it with her assistance. I tuck my legs under me and glance up at the hole that she's watching, wondering what I'm supposed to see. "Did you...need another smoke hole?" I ask, teasing.

She looks over at me, startled, then laughs. "No, no smoke hole. It is just a mistake." She sighs heavily and then glances down, rubbing her face. I notice that her hand—strikingly long and elegant compared to my own small one—is trembling.

My concern for her intensifies. "Asha, what is it?" I touch her arm. "What's wrong?" When she hesitates, I say, "You can tell me, you know. I'm your friend. I won't say anything to anyone if you don't want me to."

She nods slowly and looks down at her lap, clasping her hands there. "It is not a bad thing, Claire. Do not worry. I just...I do not know what to think of it."

"What is it? Can you tell me?" I think of her missing mate. "Is it Hemalo? Did you fight?"

Asha gives a small snort. "I wish. We..." She glances down, takes a deep breath, and then looks over at me. "We resonated again."

I sit back, rocked by this reveal. Holy cow. "Oh, girl." I reach for her hand and squeeze it. "You must be a mess right now."

She sniffs and then swipes at her face, brushing away tears with her free hand. "I like that you are not telling me to be excited. Any sa-khui would tell me that I should be pleased."

"Humans are not so black and white," I reply with a pat on her knee. "We don't automatically think that just because the cootie decides you should mate with someone that you should be thrilled about it."

Her quick smile tells me I'm on the right track. She's anxious about things with Hemalo.

"You hate him?" I guess aloud. "And you don't want to be pulled back into a mating with him?"

"I do not hate him," Asha says softly. "I am sad he has abandoned me. I am sad he no longer wants to be mated to me. I know I was not a good mate to him. I pushed him away when he tried to be kind, and eventually he decided to stop trying."

"But now you have resonated again."

Her lip trembles. "And I worry it will all go wrong again. That my body will not be able to carry my kit, and we will hate each other once more." Her hand covers mine and clenches it tightly. "I do not think I can bear to go through that again."

My poor friend. I put my arms around her and hug her. She is stiff in my grasp, but then relaxes and puts her head on my shoulder. "It's all right to worry about this sort of thing, you know. It happened, and it was terrible." I rub her back. "It's something no one should have to go through."

"My world ended when Hashala died." Asha's voice is stark with grief. "She died, and when Hemalo tried to comfort me, I pushed him away. I did not know how to handle it. I still do not. At first I tried to ignore it. If I did not think about it, maybe it would not hurt." Her throat works as if she is trying to swallow a knot. "Hemalo did not understand why I was not grieving like him. So I was cold to him. I said ugly things." She sighs heavily. "And I tried to mate other males. I thought maybe I should hurt him like I was hurting."

Eek. Things just got awkward. I suspected as much given Kira's coolness to Asha, but hearing it said aloud is tricky. I pat her back. "You were trying to find a way to make it hurt less. I understand."

"No one took me up on my offer. I was still mated, of course. If I was not mated, I could have a dozen males in as many nights. But you never touch the mate of another." She snorts. "Not that my mate wanted me at that point. He has not touched me since Hashala was born, and that was many seasons ago."

"You said yourself you were cruel to him. I imagine he was hurt, too." I keep my tone as non-judgmental as possible. I doubt Asha's ever confessed all this hurt and pain to anyone, and I don't want her to think she can't talk to me. I'm aching for her, because I know what it's like to feel alone and friendless and terrified, and to hurt. To have everything you love pulled away from you in an instant. We humans have settled in well enough, but I still grieve Earth and its beaches, a warm day of scorching hot sunshine. A pizza fresh from the oven. Chocolate. A movie or a day at the mall. My parents and my dog, even though they were dead by the time I got snatched by aliens. I still miss them. I still miss all of it.

"I still hurt. Every day, I hurt for her." She reaches into the furs and pulls out a tunic for a baby. It's so tiny. She pulls it to her face and presses it to her mouth, then inhales deeply. "It no longer smells like her. I wish it did. She was so..." Her voice catches. "Perfect."

My eyes sting with tears. She's carrying around so much grief. "I know."

"I should have carried her for another season," Asha whispers. "But she came anyhow, and she was so small. So very small. Even this fit her like a blanket." She strokes the tiny tunic. "She was too fragile to accept a khui. You have to be healthy and strong, otherwise it takes too much and…" She chokes on the words. "Hashala…she…she couldn't."

"It's okay," I tell her softly. "I know how much she meant to you. Losing her doesn't mean that you're wrong for grieving her. You're going to miss her every single day, and that's all right. There's nothing wrong with that."

She sits up. "I am scared, Claire. What if my body will not hold another kit? What if I fulfill resonance with Hemalo and my kit comes early again? What if I ruin another life?" Her hands go to her stomach. "What if my khui does not realize that I cannot have a kit and just keeps making me resonate over and over again and—"

"Stop it," I tell her gently. "You're panicking. You are strong. You're healthy, and so is Hemalo."

"But I was healthy last time."

"And something happened. I can't change that." I take her hand and give it a sympathetic squeeze. "But it doesn't mean it will happen this time. And it doesn't mean that there is something wrong with you. If there was, don't you think Maylak would have seen it and fixed it?"

"I want to believe you. I do. But I am frightened."

"Of course you're frightened. That's normal. Anyone would be, in your place. But look at how many kits have been born—"

"Human kits," she interjects.

"And Maylak has two healthy children," I reply. "They are fully sa-khui and fine. And there are kits born every day on this planet. Look at how many metlaks there are out there."

She snorts. "Those are animals. Beasts."

"I don't know about the metlak," I say thoughtfully. "They might just be furry people. Furry, very smelly people."

"Beasts," she says imperiously.

I shrug. "So what if they are? They are born healthy. Birth is a natural thing, my friend. Your kit will be fine."

"But what if mine is not fine?" Her face is full of fear.

"But what if it is?" I counter. "You will never know unless you try."

"Oh, I must try." Asha rolls her eyes in a very human expression. "Resonance will not allow me to say no."

"Do you want to say no?" I ask. Even on this primitive planet, with a healer, if she doesn't want her baby, maybe there's a way to fix that for her, even though my heart hurts at the thought.

She is silent for a very long time, her gaze focused on the hole in the ceiling as if it will provide her with answers. Then she looks over at me. "I want a kit more than anything else in the world. I am so tired of my arms being empty."

"Then you have to take a chance," I encourage her. "Talk to Hemalo. I'm sure he's scared, too, because I'm betting that he's worried about the same things you are. But you guys can lean on each other instead of drifting apart. This is a sign that you're meant to have a family, Asha. You can't let Hashala's death destroy you and any happiness you might ever have. You deserve to be happy. You deserve to have a kit and a mate. You deserve all these things. But going after what you want will mean taking a chance."

Asha nods slowly. "I am scared."

"Girl, if you weren't scared, you wouldn't be human." I put my arm around her shoulders and pull her in for another hug, ignoring the fact that the bony plates on her arms scratch at my skin.

A laugh bubbles up from her throat. “I am not human. Not in the slightest.”

“All right,” I amend with a grin. “You would not be sa-khui.”

9

ASHA

Claire is wise. I think about her words as she feeds fuel to the fire and makes me tea. She should be out spending the day singing songs and enjoying the haw-lee-day with the tribe, but she is here with me in my hut. She is a good friend, and I am so grateful for her presence that I nearly start to weep again. I am a mess of emotions this day, it seems.

The resonance thrums in my breast, reminding me that it has not been fulfilled. Last time I resonated, I took Hemalo to my furs immediately. It feels strange to delay things, like I am not doing this right. Is my kit even now inside me, waiting for us to mate so it can begin to grow? It is a strange thought, and I touch my stomach. Hemalo has not come by, and I wonder if he is agonizing like I am. Probably. He is a thinker, Hemalo. He will not say much, but I know his mind is always working, going over everything. He will be thinking about Hashala, and the new kit.

Will he want a male or a female? Will he think of Hashala as my stomach grows? Or will the new kit replace all the aching love I have for her? I worry that I will forget her. That if a new kit fills my arms and my heart, I will have nothing left for the kit I have lost. But maybe...maybe Hemalo can help me remember.

As I muse quietly to myself, Claire moves around my howse. She dips her small finger into the pouch and pulls back with an exclamation at how hot it is. She moves to the cupboard where Farli keeps our dishes and pulls out a pair of shiny new bone cups. I realize as she pours tea that those must be Farli's cups, not mine. I have made no effort to replace anything that I lost in the earth-shake. That will not do. Not if I am to have a kit. Not if I am to cave with Hemalo again. Not if we are to be a family once more. Farli will have to return to her mother's hearth or keep the howse to herself. I wonder if Hemalo has a howse in the vee-lage or if he will move into mine. I muse on the thought as I sip the tea and Claire chatters about the haw-lee-day. I know she is trying to distract me, and so I smile and pretend to listen.

Perhaps...perhaps this is a good thing.

I am still terrified, of course. The thought of spending endless seasons pregnant again, only to lose the thing I want most in the world? It breaks my heart. But...resonance chooses when the kits are born, and to whom. We do not choose. I cannot fight it, because in the end, I will give in. The khui controls all. It does not make me angry, strangely enough. I know some of the humans have fought hard against resonance—Jo-see and Haeden spring to mind. In the end, the khui always wins.

If I knew Hemalo wanted this—wanted me—then I think I could bear it a bit more. I could stand the terror and the fear if it felt like we were in this together. But his words yesterday hurt me down to my core. Telling me that we did not have to act right away? Acting as if this is unimportant? He should know how I feel.

I truly do not think he wishes to be with me. I fret over this as I drink my tea. Once, I thought he was devoted to me despite my unfairness to him. Perhaps he has truly given up, and not even resonance can salvage what is between us. The thought makes me sad. I picture us together, as a family, laughing and smiling around a fire, cozy during the worst storms that the brutal season can bring down upon us. I think of him as the father to my kit, holding the child and tossing it into the air as Vektal does to his little Talie. My heart feels warm. He would be a good father.

Now that my initial terror is ebbing, I am starting to grow excited.

Resonance means a new kit to love. A new life to carry and nurture. I have never wanted anything more than I have wanted this. And while it will not bring Hashala back to me, it will let me try again. Perhaps this time, I will be the mother I have wanted to be. I will get to hold my own kit close to my breast and love it, instead of holding someone else's and wishing. The new kit will not take the place of the one I lost, but to have my own...oh. Just the thought is a dream. I touch my flat stomach and think about it with wonder.

Unless something goes wrong...

"I see that look on your face," Claire says between sips. "Stop it, Asha. You're just torturing yourself."

"It is just...what if something goes wrong?"

"My mother always said that worrying about what might happen does nothing but make you crazy." She finishes her tea and puts down her cup. "So, is there a reason why you're still sitting here with me and not talking to Hemalo?"

I set my tea aside and draw my legs up, hugging them close. "You push hard."

"I'm your friend. I want what's best for you. And sitting on this isn't going to help things."

"He could come and talk to me, too," I point out.

"He could, but he hasn't, and there must be a reason for that," Claire says. "Maybe he's waiting for you to make the first move. Maybe he thinks you're upset and doesn't want to upset you more. Or maybe he's being a big chicken. Whatever it is, you'll never know unless you go and speak to him."

"Shick-un?" I ask.

Claire waves a hand in the air. "You know what I mean. Quit stalling. Go talk to him!"

"And say what?"

"Tell him how you feel!"

I think for a moment and then sigh, hugging my legs close. "I am not sure how I feel, Claire."

"Which is also not the worst thing to tell him. I imagine he's feeling a little conflicted himself." She gets up from her seat and picks up our teacups. "I'll clean up here. You go talk to him."

My gut clenches, the nervous feeling bubbling over. What if he says cruel things? What if he does not want to give mating with me another try? What if he will mate with me but pushes me away again? Then I will have to go through all of this alone. The thought is terrifying, but not undeserved. I have been hard to love. I might have destroyed any hope for the future with my actions.

But it is as Claire says—I will never know unless I go and speak to Hemalo.

I suck in a deep breath. Get to my feet. I straighten my tunic and run a hand over my mane, feeling nervous. If he says cruel things, I will not be able to bear it. I feel as fragile as one of the humans right now.

"You look beautiful. Go!"

"Going," I mutter. I grab a warm wrap and fling it over my shoulders, then push the flap aside and step out into the air. The chill is bone-deep, despite it being midday. I glance up at the sky out of habit, and it looks as if the storm is abating, which means the hunters will be able to go out tomorrow. The next day of celebrations—coloring eggs and hiding them around the vee-lage for some reason—will have to wait. I wrap my fur tighter around my body and head toward the howse that the unmated hunters live in. It is on the far end of the vee-lage, and I pass many empty, lidless howses as I walk. Perhaps when all the new kits in the tribe are grown up, they will live in these.

And perhaps my kit will be amongst them.

The thought is an encouraging one, and I quicken my steps. I need to talk to Hemalo. To get to an understanding with him. To see how I can make him stop hating me so much so we can mate and bring resonance full circle.

And bring our kit one step closer to death, possibly. I hate that the thought echoes in my mind, but I cannot stop it. The fear will be with me, always, lurking like a shadow.

I must not think about that. Not now.

This end of the vee-lage is quiet, and the only sound is the distant echo of laughter and singing at the long-howse and the endless howling of the wind above. There is no sound of Hemalo working his hides. Those are sounds I know well—the wet slap of the brain-mash on the leather, or the scrape of his bone tool along a hide. Is he not working, then? Sleeping?

I move to his leather-working hut, but it is empty, his tools neatly put away, skins rolled up. No work today, then. Is he sick? Has resonance made him ill enough that he cannot leave his bed? The thought fills me with concern—and floods me with arousal at the same time. It has been a long time since Hemalo has touched me, and I miss it. Of all of my fur-partners, he was my last...and the best one. He would always make sure I was pleasured hard and pleasured well, but my favorite part was how he held me close afterward, as if he could not bear to let me go. I want that again. Even now, I grow slick between my thighs thinking about it, and the tip of my tail tingles with excitement. I have not felt like mating in a very, very long time, and yet it seems to consume my thoughts right now. It is the resonance, I know, but it gives me hope. It makes me feel... normal again. Like I am not completely dead inside.

I like that.

The howse the hunters occupy has the privacy flap pulled back. I peek inside, but it is empty, too. Hmm. Did Hemalo join the celebration, after all? I turn and head back toward the long-howse, fighting back my nervousness. Is he avoiding me? The thought sparks a flash of irritation, and I stomp toward the gathering.

But when I get there and peer inside...he is not there, either.

Where is he?

My skin prickles with awareness. This is not right. This is not like Hemalo. He would not be petty. I leave the gathering before anyone can invite me to stay, and race back toward the hunters' dwelling. When I make it back, I move through the howse, gauging belongings. That pile of messy furs belongs to Harrec, and that one is Taushen's, judging by the spear nearby. This one is Warrek's, and this one, Bek. None of the furs belong to Hemalo, who always has the softest, best-made furs in the entire tribe. I do not see the basket that holds his things, either. I do not see his rarely used spear, or the skinning knife that his father gave him.

He is not here.

He is gone. He's left.

I stare about the howse numbly. He cannot leave, can he? Not when we have resonated? It is a call that must be answered. There is no avoiding it.

And yet...Jo-see and Haeden delayed their resonance by a full turn of the moons because Jo-see ran away. She told one of the other females that it was still bad, but bearable.

Is that what Hemalo has done? He has left me behind? Shock gives way to outrage as I think about what he said to me yesterday. We do not have to decide anything just yet. Of course nothing had to be decided...because he was never planning on staying.

Once again, he has abandoned me.

It hurts. It hurts and it makes me furious all at once. How dare he? How dare he not want me or this kit? How dare he run away instead of facing the problem? Is he trying to teach me a lesson? I snarl at the empty spot where his furs should be and turn on my heel, storming back to my own howse.

Claire is still there, banking the fire. She straightens, surprised to see me. "Back already? What happened?"

"Hemalo is gone," I bite out. I move to my own furs and begin to roll them up.

"Gone? You mean he left the village?" Her voice is incredulous. "After you guys resonated?"

"It seems so." Even the thought makes my head fill with fury. When I see him again, I am going to lash him with my tongue for hours.

"But...I don't understand." She moves to my side, a question in her eyes. "How can they let him go? Isn't it dangerous?"

"The weather is easing," I say, bundling my furs tight before lashing a cord around them. "He must have seen the break in the clouds and decided to take a chance."

"That idiot!" Claire exclaims.

I nod.

She looks down at my hands and then frowns up at me. "What are you doing?"

I bare my teeth in a half-smile, half-feral-snarl. He thinks to run away from me? No chance. "I am going after him."

10

HEMALO

Next Day

I think of Asha as I stroke my cock, my hand braced on a nearby rock for support.

It is probably not wise to stand in the midst of a valley in the brutal season, my leggings down around my ankles, my cock as stiff as a spear in my hand, but resonance will not allow me to continue walking unless I sate the urge to mate. So I continue, working my hand up and down the length roughly. I close my eyes, imagining her sultry eyes and the throaty way she laughs as I enter her. I imagine her wet heat clenching tight around my length—

—And my seed spurts into the snow, so hot that it hisses and steams as it hits. I kick a bit of new snow over the evidence of my need, noting that it has changed to a thick, milky substance instead of the thin liquid I normally ejaculate. It is yet another sign that resonance has its grip tight on my body.

How in all of the snows did Haeden and his mate manage to avoid mating for nearly a full moon? It has been almost two days and I feel as if all the blood in my body—and all the sensation—has flooded to my cock and lodged there permanently. Everything bothers me—the brush of leather against my skin, the feel of the wind rustling against my tail, the hard surface of the rock under my hand—it all makes my cock stir and respond as if it has a life of its own. It is miserable.

Sometimes I think I should turn back to the vee-lage and speak to Asha, but I cannot. I do not want to torture her. Until she has time to adjust to our newest resonance, I must stay away from her.

I miss her, though. I miss her like I would miss my own tail. Her absence is an ache behind my heart...and a constant ache in my groin. But it is for her that I do this. I do not want her to feel pressured. I do not want her to feel as if I am forcing her into a decision, or that I do not respect the grief she still carries for our little Hashala. So away I go.

I adjust my clothing and then pick up my spear again, using it as a walking stick. Though I do not hunt as much as the others, I am capable of taking care of myself out on the trails. I am not much with my spear, but I am good with snares and traps, and I can catch my own food for a time and work the skins. My chief was not pleased with my decision to leave, but he understood why. He knows as well as I do that Asha is sensitive and her grief for our lost kit has been overwhelming. He worries over her, too. Vektal's mate, Shorshie, gave me a bag of dried meat for my journey and will deliver the rest of my 'secret presents' to Maylak so the healer is not left wanting simply because I am not there to play the game.

The weather is awful, the skies clearing just enough that snow does not pound my face constantly as I walk. It lies thick on the ground, though, at waist height in some areas. It makes walking slow and any travel cold and unpleasant. The nearest hunter cave is a day or so away at the pace I am making, but I am in no hurry. I will set up camp there, work on refilling the nearest cache, and skin for hour after endless hour to waste the time. When I can stand it no longer, then I will return.

Hopefully by then, Asha will realize that our second resonance is a gift and not something to be frightened of. Then she will accept me with open arms and a smile, and we will try again.

I walk onward, trying to turn my thoughts away from Asha. I think of the cold snow caking onto my boots, and the fact that I will have a long, chilly night ahead. I must either build a big fire to keep the breath from turning to ice in my lungs, or keep moving through the night so I do not freeze into an icicle. I should concentrate on that and the deadly cold. Instead, I am thinking about Asha. Does she think about me? About the kit we might make together?

Or are her thoughts more...passionate in nature? I envision her in her furs, her fingers sliding back and forth over her slick, dusky-blue folds. They will be wet with arousal, the scent of her perfuming the air. She will have the tip of her tail in her mouth, unable to resist the additional pleasure that a tiny bite on the end will give her.

I stop and shudder. A groan escapes me, and my cock is already hard and aching once more.

Think of something else, I command myself. Anything.

I think of leather and leatherworking. I think of Asha lying on the skins I am working on, pouting and begging me to put my mouth on her cunt even as she spreads her long legs for me.

That…is not working. I try to think of hunting instead. Animals. Dvisti. Snowcats. Setting snares.

Instead, I think of Asha and the way she lets her tail lash around my arm when I put my mouth on her cunt and lick her.

Curse the weather. I grit my teeth and grab at the waistband of my leggings again, untying the knot so I can pull my cock out and stroke it once more.

Perhaps it is because I am so focused on Asha that I do not hear the footsteps behind me until it is too late. Something hard hits my head, and then I see a flash of dirty white fur before I hit the ground.

CLAIRE

"It's been four days. Should we go after them?" I toy with the decorative knots on the edge of my new tunic, worried.

Megan slaps at my hands. "Quit fussing. You're going to ruin that pretty new tunic that Sevvah made for you."

I stick my tongue out at her, momentarily distracted from my all-consuming worry over Asha. "I wish she was the one giving me all the other gifts."

"Still?" Georgie asks, glancing over at me. She pulls Pacy's bone dreidel out of Talie's hands and gives it back to the little boy.

I'm sitting by the fire early this morning with the others while Stacy makes us a 'holiday' breakfast of eggs and not-potato latkes. Feast Day isn't until the next day—today is Family Day, which means exchanging gifts with family and spending a meal with them. Kinda a quasi-Thanksgiving, sa-khui style. Except they've all thrown themselves into the whole gift-giving situation and everyone's been handing gifts out right and left to anyone and everyone. It's sweet, and I love that everyone's into the holiday...

But it's also making it that much harder to find out who my secret gift-giver is. Ugh.

I suppose I should be thankful that I'm still getting the mystery gifts. Between those and the celebrations (and my affectionate, marvelous mate being around), it's almost serving to distract me from the fact that Asha and Hemalo have been gone for days. I get up from my stool and head over to the rolled-back awning in the longhouse, glancing out. The weather is super foul today, but of course it is. If it wasn't, Ereven wouldn't be sitting by the fireside, letting Farli and Sessah paint swirls all over his forearms like a big blue sa-khui canvas. "I worry about them," I tell Georgie and Megan. "You think we should send someone after them?"

"Nope," Georgie says in a confident voice. She grabs Talie before she can steal Pacy's dreidel again and hands her a new toy—a woven basket with a lid. "They're fine, I promise."

"But how do you know?" I move back toward the women, still worried.

"Um, because they lived on this planet for hundreds of years before we got here and the cold doesn't bother them like it does us? This isn't their first winter, and it won't be their last. They know how to take care of themselves. They're fine."

"Georgie's right," Megan says, rubbing the back of her little one as it nurses. "You're stressing out over nothing. Enjoy the day, girl. Isn't that what today is all about? Relaxing and enjoying ourselves? You're the only one not relaxing!"

I doubt I'm the only one. But I sigh and sit back down again. "But what if—"

"Nope," Georgie interjects before I can say more. She's got her 'chief's mate' voice going now. "Leave it alone, Claire. I promise you, they're fine. Someone going after them would just make it worse. And do you really want to send someone away chasing those two bickering dorks when there's hunting to be done? Do you want Ereven or any of the other hunters to miss out on the celebrations only to find Asha and Hemalo bickering—"

"And humping," Megan adds quickly.

"—in the snow?"

I roll my eyes. "Fine, fine. I'm being a worrywart."

"You are," Georgie agrees with a smile. "But it's sweet that you're concerned. You're being a good friend to Asha."

She's been a good friend to me, too. I wouldn't have half of the stuff organized if it weren't for her help, and she knew just how to approach people to make them excited about silly human customs. Even if she doesn't believe it sometimes, people in this tribe care about her and love her. They want what's best for her.

Including me.

"Claire?" Warrek asks, moving to my side. He's got a basket in his hands.

"Oh no," Megan moans, a horrified laugh escaping her throat. "Another?"

I gasp, getting slowly to my feet. "Warrek, is it you?"

"No," the quiet hunter says. He has such an awkward look on his face that I feel a stab of pity for him. "I was only told to deliver it. I promise."

I narrow my eyes at him and then cross my arms over my chest, resting them just over my baby bump. "What if I don't want it?"

He glances over at the far end of the longhouse and then back to me. "I...uh..."

Oooh. So the gift-giver is still nearby? "They're here, aren't they?"

Warrek shakes his head, a panicked look moving over his features. "No. I did not say that."

"You don't have to." I use Megan's shoulder to brace myself, and maneuver my way through the crowd of people. I head for the entrance, because that's where Warrek was looking. Sure enough, as I move to the entrance of the longhouse, I see a figure cloaked in furs hurrying away back down the main street of Croatoan village. Hmm. I look around the fire once more, but my mate is here. My friends are here. Who is it?

Ereven looks over at me, curious. I raise a finger at him, indicating I'll be just a moment, and then head out of the lodge after my mysterious gift-giver. Time to figure out who it is.

I can't exactly hurry after the person, but there's only so many places one can hide in our little village. I know where to go, and so I head down the main street, then look for smoke plumes. My gift-giver's gotten a little careless, and now I'm going to have her. Or him. The figure disappears into a hut at the far end of the village, the only one with a trickle of smoke from the teepee top of the house. I recognize the house, too. I slow down as I approach, not wanting to scare off my furtive friend. As I move toward the house, I see the privacy flap is up, and I enter, ready to confront the person.

It's exactly who I thought it was. The moment I saw the house, I knew. And the person that looks up when I enter isn't the least bit surprised to see me.

It's Bek.

11

ASHA

I am lucky that I have the fire burning in my belly to keep me warm. After days of chasing Hemalo's tracks, I am tired, cold, and hungry. I am even more annoyed with him for leaving me behind, and hurt that he would do such a thing without even trying to talk to me.

I am also incredibly, irritatingly aroused. The soft fur of my thickest tunic only serves to rub against my sensitive skin and drive home the fact that I have resonated and have no way to relieve myself of this need. When I find Hemalo, I am going to tear his hide up, I decide, for making me trek all over the hills looking for him.

And then I hope he wants to go straight into the furs.

Actually, do I even want that? My heart is still torn. He has abandoned me—twice now—and yet my body craves his. I want the kit our resonance will bring, as much as it terrifies me to think I could lose another. If I must do this—and resonance says I must—I need my mate at my side. I need his quiet strength to lean on. Without it, I am just an endless fire of rage, burning myself and others as I struggle to come to grips with my grief. I need him.

In return, I will be...kinder. I will not lash out at him as much when I hurt, I decide. I will try to be a better mate. It will be a struggle, but all good things are worth more effort. I only hope that Hemalo sees me as something still worth the effort. Perhaps he does not. Perhaps this is why he has abandoned me again.

Even as I think about it, the helpless anger that has burned in my gut for days, ever since I found him gone, stirs forth once more. Why leave without talking? Why not speak to me? Tell me what he feels instead of just leaving? I hate that I must guess. I assume I know what is in his heart—are we not closer than anyone else in the tribe?

And yet...he has left me. So I do not know him at all, and it makes me furious. Does he think I like being angry all the time? Or sad? I want to be normal. I want to be happy. I need his help to regain my grip on happiness. His absence feels all wrong. It has since the moment he left me.

I am stomping now, I realize, as I trudge through the snow. Stomping because thinking about everything makes me feel angry, frustrated, and helpless all at once. My future is in his grip and he will not even talk to me, I grumble to myself as I move through the path forged in the snow. At least his trail is easy to follow. There has been no new snowfall, and the suns have even peeked out from behind the thick cloud cover, letting the gouge Hemalo has carved into the hip-deep snow crust over. I have seen no sign of him yet, but I suspect I am close. The trail grows fresher by the hour.

I pause and inhale the cold air, glancing around. The trail merges with another trail a short distance away, which is puzzling. Did he meet another hunter? But everyone was back at the vee-lage, so that cannot be it. Perhaps he ran across a dvisti and went after it? But the trails are wrong. It is almost as if someone saw Hemalo's trail and then began to follow him. Strange.

The nearest hunter cave is in the next valley, very close to where I am. Perhaps he went there. I move a little faster, getting out my bone knife, just in case.

A moment later, I see a flash of blue up ahead. It is no more than a dot in the distance, but I recognize the shade of Hemalo's skin. Aha. Encouraged, I walk faster, my khui beginning a loud, pleasant song at the realization that my mate is close. I try to think of the words to say to him now that I have caught him. Before I left, Claire advised me to be calm, to tell him my thoughts without being accusing. I have had long hours to think of what to say, but everything I planned has disappeared from my mind.

All I can think is 'you left me.' You left me.

The angry fire burning in my belly once more, I storm forward, but as I do, I notice that the blue mound in the distance is not moving forward. I grow closer to it with every step. It also does not look as tall as Hemalo, though that is the dusky blue of his skin. Is he...sitting?

The snow moves near him as I approach, and I realize he is not alone a moment before the smell of metlak touches my nostrils. The panic I have been fighting surges inside me, fiercer than any rage. I run forward, screaming, brandishing my knife.

The metlak crouching near him in the snow rises, tall and impossibly thin. It holds a rock in one hand, the surface glossy with frozen blood. A second shape rises—another metlak. It is holding Hemalo's bag.

Hemalo does not move. He lies on the snow, completely still.

Fear shivers through me, and I bellow louder, surging forward.

He cannot be dead.

He *cannot.*

I choke back my grief and slash wildly at the air. "Get away from him!" I stand over my fallen mate, brandishing my knife. I want to check him to see if he is breathing, but I cannot take my eyes off of the two wild creatures. I snag one of the straps on his pack and jerk it toward me, out of the grip of the metlak's hands.

The awful, smelly creatures shy back a few steps, hissing at me. The smaller one crouches low again, moving awkwardly, and reaches for the bag.

I jerk it out of reach and slash at the other one. Its face is covered in matted fur, and one round eye glares balefully at me as it hoots and hisses a warning. I hiss back and slash at it again. "Leave! He is mine!"

They creep backward a few steps, and then hover, waiting. My fear and rage boils through me, and I storm forward, slashing at the air. "Leave this place! Go!"

When I lunge forward, the bigger one-eyed metlak swipes at me with his claws, and I duck away. They keep eyeing Hemalo's pack, and it is clear to me they do not want to leave without it... or without Hemalo. The big one claws at me again. I move automatically, jerking my knife downward and connect with flesh and bone and fur. My blade bounces off its arm, and blood sprays into the snow, the foul scent of the metlak growing stronger.

The creature howls in pain, and they both scamper away, abandoning us and the pack.

I gasp for breath, excited and terrified all at once. “Hemalo?” I crouch low by him, scanning the snow even as I touch his neck, looking for a pulse.

It is there, and I sob with relief. Good. Very good. I stroke his cheek and then get back to my feet, cautious. Where there is one metlak, there are always more, and glance around, looking for others. When a few moments pass and no new creatures arrive to attack us, I swing my gaze back to the two attackers. They are far away now, still loping across the snow at full speed. They will not return. Not soon. They are cowardly creatures, but these two were bolder than most.

I must get Hemalo out of here before they return with more. I wipe my now-bloody knife off on my tunic and then return it to its sheath before kneeling at Hemalo’s side once more. I examine his face, touching his cheek and tracing over his skin. There is a large, bloody wound in his mane where they struck him with the rock, and a few claw marks on his arms and shoulders where they grabbed at his pack, but he is otherwise unharmed. I am so relieved. I touch his face again, brushing my fingers over his lips. “I have you,” I whisper. “Do not worry.”

I pull my pack apart, looking for my extra leggings. When I find them, I tear them apart at the seams and then use the long strips of leather to bind his head wound tightly. It does not look grievous, but I worry that the healer is not here to fix it. “I cannot lose you, too,” I tell him. “So you do not get to die on me.”

Hemalo makes no answer, not that I expected one.

I check him over for wounds one more time. The scratches are ugly but not deep, and icing over already. I need to get him to a warm fire, shelter, and clean the filth out of the cuts. At least the hunter cave is close. There, I can take care of my mate.

"You are lucky you did not resonate to one of the puny humans," I tell his unconscious body as I put our packs back together and bundle them into one large burden that I sling over my shoulder. Then I slide an arm under Hemalo's back and under his legs and lift him into the air, carrying him as I would a child. He is bulky, but not too heavy for me, and I am heartened when his khui begins to sing loudly to mine.

Soon, I tell it.

The winds grow blustery by the time I get to the cave, dark clouds on the horizon. A storm will be rolling in overnight, which means more snow and more bone-chillingly cold weather. The cave is dark and reeks of metlak, which makes me worry. I set Hemalo down in the entrance and then creep inside with my knife to investigate, but all is quiet inside. If the metlaks were here, they are gone now. I return to the fire pit and build a roaring fire quickly, and then check to make sure there is enough fuel to last several days if necessary. I do not want to go chasing down frozen dvisti dung if there is a snowstorm. Luckily, the cave is well stocked, if a mess. It is clear to me that the metlaks came inside and tore through the supplies here. They left the furs and fuel alone, but the stored food has been demolished, the small baskets upturned and the contents spilled everywhere. There is metlak scat in the far corner of the double-cave, and it stinks almost as much as a metlak does. Faugh.

It looks like I will be spending the next several hours cleaning up their mess. I rub a hand under my nose as if that will block the smell, and then move Hemalo close to the fire. I tuck a blanket around him and make him comfortable while I wait for him to awaken. It might be hours. It might be…never. I do not like to think about that, though. He is strong in body and breathing well. There is no reason to panic. I fight the swell of fear down and force myself to remain busy. If he will be out for hours, I can clean and make the cave habitable again.

It is a good plan. I take several deep, calming breaths and place my hand over my heart, where my khui is singing frantically. Not yet, I tell it. As much as I want resonance to happen, I also do not wish to climb atop my unconscious mate and use his body. The thought is revolting. I want him to be present with me. I want him to look into my eyes as we make our kit. With a sigh, I get to my feet and pick up one of the baskets. It has been torn apart, the dried meat inside filthy and uneaten. Such a waste. Metlaks are filthy creatures, though, and I will not chance eating something they have pawed. I toss the entire basket into the fire and watch it burn for a moment before turning back to do more cleaning.

As I clean, I think about the tribe. Stay-see and Pashov were in this cave recently. The human female mentioned that they had stayed in a large cave with two chambers, and that is this cave. She mentioned that the cave had been visited by a metlak, though it did not stay for long. Perhaps it keeps coming back because it knows there is food here. I will have to tell Vektal, and if this cave is being used by metlaks, it is no longer safe to use for hunters. We will be safe as long as there is a fire, but…I move to the front of the cave and push the privacy screen over the entrance, just in case. Not that a metlak would honor it, but I feel better with it there.

I return to the back of the cave and eye the messy piles, contemplating what to tackle next. Then something chirps.

I am utterly still.

The cave is silent. I relax a bit. Did I imagine the sound, then? It is like nothing I have ever heard before, and I mentally run through the list of small, burrowing creatures that might have invaded a sa-khui cave to escape the brutal season.

The chirp happens again.

It is coming from the back of the cave, where the metlaks have made the biggest mess. Curious, I move slowly forward. There's a large pile of debris made from food remnants, filth, and what looks to be tufts of metlak hair pushed into a pile. Lying atop this mess is a rounded ball of dirty fluff with wiggling arms and big, round eyes. It sees me, and the thin arms move and it chirps again.

A metlak kit.

I am too shocked to make a sound. Is this why the metlaks are at this cave? Because there is a kit? But this kit is far too thin to be healthy. I slowly reach over and pick it up, and it makes a happier-sounding chirp at me. The thing smells, and its fur is matted with filth, but it is young and hungry. "What do I do with you?" I whisper to it.

The kit wriggles in my arms and makes another chirping sound, this one hungrier than the last. Its little beak-like mouth moves, and the big eyes blink at me. They glow a bright blue, just like my Hashala's did.

I...do not know what to do. I have always been taught that metlaks are pests to be driven away. They will not hesitate to kill a hunter, and our hunters do not hesitate to kill them in return. The adults are filthy, mean, and dangerous.

But this is a kit, not even a full season old. It is filthy like an adult metlak, but it is not mean or dangerous. I pull it close to my tunic, and it burrows against me for warmth, and my heart hurts as it starts rooting about, searching for a teat. It is starving. The kindest thing to do would be to put it out in the snow and let the frost make short work of it.

I...cannot do that.

I tuck it against my shoulder, stroking the matted hair. "Why did your mother leave you? Is it too hard for her to hunt with you at her side?" I think of the two metlaks standing over Hemalo. They were desperate to get his pack. Have those two now realized that sa-khui caves - and sa-khui hunters have supplies? Are they hungry enough to attack a hunter in hopes of food?

I pick my way back toward the fire, frowning at the nearly full basket of dried meat burning there. They did not eat this, and they were starving. Do they only eat roots, then? "Perhaps you'd like a root broth," I tell the little one as I move toward the fire.

It chirps hungrily at me again, as if it can understand me.

I rub its small back, and a wave of stink rises.

I need lots of water, then. Some for tea for my mate for when he awakens. Some for a broth to feed this tiny, smelly kit. And some for a bath. I also need to finish cleaning the cave and take stock of the supplies, as well as keep the fire going. It seems like an overwhelming amount of things to do for one person.

And yet...I feel invigorated. I feel alive. Happy. This kit needs me. My mate needs me. Perhaps Hemalo is not the only one that has needed a purpose recently.

Smiling, I tuck the kit against my shoulder and get to work.

12

HEMALO

Something smells foul, so foul it rouses me from my sleep and a ringing headache. I am disoriented, but even with my eyes closed, the smells and sounds are familiar. Well, most of the smells. I smell smoke through the stink, and feel the soft down of fur against my skin. I hear the crackling of fire, and Asha's soft, tuneless humming, the rumble in my chest as my khui sings to hers—all of these are familiar and comforting.

But I open my eyes, because something about this is not right. My eyes slowly focus, and I see a rock ceiling above me and not a teepee. A cave. I am in a cave. How did I get here? I search my memories, but my last ones are of travel, and slogging through thick snow. Have I forgotten part of my trip? Is this why my head aches so?

My cock aches, too. I realize this even as it occurs to me that my khui is singing, and quite loudly. I look over, and there is Asha by the fire, a bundle cradled in her arms and a lovely smile on her face.

My mate. My sweet, beautiful, fiery mate. I am filled with a fierce joy at the sight of her happiness, but as I study her and the leather-covered bundle she cuddles close, fear shoots through me. Is that...our kit? I touch my brow. Have I fallen victim to the same problem that Pashov did? Have I been struck on the head and forgotten the last few turns? Panic surges through me, and I sit upright quickly. The swift action makes my head pound in response, and I press my hand to the base of my horns, groaning.

"Hemalo," Asha murmurs in a soft voice. "Are you well?"

"I do not know...I... Asha, have I forgotten our kit? Have I forgotten seasons like Pashov did?"

She blinks at me, surprised, and then down at the bundle in her arms. Her mouth twitches in a smile, and she gives a slow shake of her head. "Do not panic. This little one is not yours."

I frown. "Then whose?" I am surprised at the vicious stab of jealousy that takes over me. She is my mate. She resonates to no one but me.

Her smile widens, and she pulls the leather away, then holds the kit out for me to see.

It is not a sa-khui kit. It is...fluffy. It is white and downy and looks like a fuzzy ball of fluff with metlak eyes and a tiny metlak beak. It chirps and coos at me even as it clings to one of Asha's braids.

"It is...a metlak?"

"A much cleaner one," Asha says, tucking it back into the blankets with affection. "The poor thing was filthy when I found it."

"What is it doing here?" I glance around me, curious. "For that matter, what are you doing here?"

"I am here because I came after you." Her smile fades, and she will not look me in the eye. She focuses on the tiny metlak instead, dipping her finger in a bowl and then putting the fingertip into the metlak kit's mouth. It licks hungrily at her, trying to feed. "And this little one was left here in this cave, probably by the metlaks that attacked you."

"Metlaks attacked me?"

"You do not remember?"

I rack my brain, trying to recall. All I remember is walking and thinking of my mate. Thinking ravenous, hungry, needy things about my mate. "Perhaps...I was distracted?"

"One hit you on the head from behind. They knocked you out." She strokes the fluffy face of the creature, gazing down at it before smiling over at me. "Does it hurt?"

It does. I touch my brow and find it covered with tight leather bindings. "I should have been more careful."

"They are starving and clever, these metlaks. I do not think you could have imagined that they would attack you to steal your pack."

She is right; that does not sound like typical metlak behavior. I frown to myself and resist the urge to rub my aching forehead as I move toward the fire to sit next to her. "Why did they want my pack?"

"I think they have been living in this cave." She gestures around her. "It was a filthy mess when I arrived, and I found this little one here. They must have left it behind to go hunting, and I think when they saw you, they assumed you would have more food. The supplies here have been eaten or ruined." She gets to her feet and hands me the bundle in her arms. "Hold him while I put fresh tea on for you."

I take the metlak kit from her, trying not to frown down at it. It is clear to me that Asha is attached to the creature. I have never liked metlaks, and like them even less now that I have been told they attacked me. But looking down at the small kit in my arms as it yawns sleepily and waves a small fist, I see why she is doting on it. Though it is ugly and covered in fur, it is a helpless kit. Asha has too soft of a heart to do anything but love it.

As if she can hear my thoughts, she moves to my side and begins to fuss with the bandages on my brow. It puts her teats at level with my eyes, and I can hear the hum of her khui through her skin. She smells like soapberries and sweat and arousal, and my cock stirs in response. I force myself to remain still while she checks my brow.

"The wound has closed," Asha says, pleased. "Good. It is swollen but should go down in a few days. You will need to get a lot of sleep. I want you feeling better as quickly as possible so we can return to the vee-lage."

She is talking as if it is already decided, which surprises me. I did not anticipate my reunion with Asha to be so...calm. I expected fire and anger. "You wish to return to the vee-lage with me? You are not mad?"

"Oh, I am furious with you," Asha says, her tone sweet despite her words. "But I am not going to yell and shake my fist at you today. Not when I thought I had lost you." She chokes on the words and then swallows hard.

I reach out and caress her tail, dragging my fingers down the smooth length of it.

She jerks out of my grip, her tail flicking angrily. "I did not say I was not mad. Do not think I have forgotten. But I am not going to spew my anger when there is a little one and you have a head injury." She casts me a heated look and then moves to the fire, grabbing her tea pouch and shaking far too many leaves into the water.

She is agitated, my mate. I hope it is because she worries over me. That is a nice thought. I cannot be mad at her subtle fury, though. This is the most...alive I have seen Asha in so many moons. Let her focus her anger on me. If it brings the spark back to her eyes, I will take it gladly.

The little one in my arms chirps, and I look down at it. It blinks at me, just like a sa-khui infant. Strange. I have never thought of the metlak as people, but I know several humans have convinced their mates that the creatures are intelligent. I do not know if I believe this, but I can see why Asha is fascinated by the kit. "It is much cleaner than its parents," I tell her absently, thinking of every other metlak I have ever seen. To a one, they are filthy, smelly creatures.

"I gave him a bath," Asha says, stirring the tea. "He smelled foul when I found him."

"And it is a boy?"

She nods, and the soft smile curves her mouth again. "I have been calling him Shasak."

I grunt. It means 'little spark.' "And what will you do with Shasak? Release him into the wild?"

"Of course not. He is a kit. He cannot take care of himself. I will keep him and protect him." When I give her an incredulous look, she shrugs. "If Farli can raise a dvisti, I can surely raise a metlak kit?"

I...have no answer for that. The idea is strange, but the humans have put a lot of strange ideas into our tribe ever since they arrived. "If it makes you happy, then you should keep it," I tell her. I will support her in this.

Her mouth twitches as she scoops tea into a cup. "I did not ask for permission. You are no longer my mate. You do not live with me. I can do as I please."

My heart sinks at her smiling words, delivered with the force of a spear-throw. "I see."

"You do not, but I do not wish to talk about it today." She moves toward me and sits down with the cup of tea, holding it gently in her hands. "Tomorrow, I will be angry at you. Today, I am grateful you are alive."

"Tomorrow, we will talk then," I say, adjusting the kit against my side and taking the cup with my free hand. "Thank you for coming after me. If you had not, I might be dead."

Her face tightens. "I know." Her hand goes to my knee and she touches me.

Just once, but it is enough for now.

She does not hate me. She is upset with me, and I sense I have hurt her, but she does not hate me. I can fix this, then. Whatever it is, I can make it better between us. And then I can claim my mate once more.

13

CLAIRE

"Bek," I say, entering the hunters' lodge. "What are you doing?"

He looks up from the spear he is sharpening, a frown on his face. "I am working on my weapons. What does it look like I am doing?"

I'm not fooled by his efforts to look busy. I know I saw him retreat into this house, and his tail is twitching too hard for me to think he's just sitting here, relaxing and working on his weapons. I call bullshit on that. "Can we talk?"

Bek shrugs and returns to work on his spear, grazing his sharpening stone along the deadly point. "What is there to say?"

Is he kidding? I have a million things to say to him. Things like, "What on earth are you doing?" and, "Why are you giving me presents when we're not mated?" and, "Don't you realize I have a resonance mate and will never be with you again?" and, "I thought you hated me," and a dozen other related questions that all bubble up in my brain. I cross my arms and study him, a bit flummoxed. I know Bek pretty well (being that we were lovers and all once upon a time), and I know that if I push at him and he doesn't want to answer, he'll just shut down entirely. I've got to steer away from accusing him. Bek has a lot of pride.

I think for a moment longer, and then decide to avoid subtlety. "Warrek's a terrible messenger, you know. He totally gave you away."

I half expect him to get annoyed, but Bek only smiles.

Then I realize it. "You sent Warrek deliberately, didn't you?" The gentle hunter has zero malice in his body, but also zero subterfuge. Warrek would be the last person I would pick to do something sneaky for me. And Bek is too clever to let his plans go off the rails because of a buddy. "You wanted to be found out."

Scraaaape. Scraaaaaape. He doesn't look up from sharpening his tools, but his tail grows more agitated.

"Do you not understand the game?" I ask gently, since he's not offering me much in the way of help. "Your secret gift person is Borran, right?"

Bek lifts his head and gives me a quick, irritated glance. "I know the rules. You have beaten them into everyone's heads repeatedly."

That's more like the prickly Bek I know. "Okay, well, if that's the case, why are you sending me gifts? You know I'm not playing."

He focuses on his spear again, shaving off a long piece of bone. "I thought you deserved something for your hard work."

I'm touched...and puzzled. And okay, I'm also a little concerned. Ever since I resonated to Ereven, Bek has left me alone. I haven't missed our relationship, because it never felt right to me, and I've been so incredibly happy with Ereven. But to hear Bek say that makes me worry he's wanting to get back together, and that could make things really darn awkward. "Ereven and I are very content," I say pointedly, and pat my pregnant belly.

"I know." He shaves another long piece off. It falls onto his thigh, and he flicks it away like it bothers him. "I have eyes."

Oookay. This is going fantastic. I continue to rub my belly. "So why...?" I can't quite somehow bring myself to confront him. "I mean..."

Bek sighs heavily, as if he didn't set this up somehow. Like it's somehow my fault, and I fight another stab of irritation at him. We always rub along like this, him and I. He gets pissy, and I cringe and avoid saying how I feel, and then we just annoy the crap out of each other until one of us can't stand it any longer. So I'm relieved when he says, "I feel guilty."

"Guilty? Why?"

He glances up at me and then gets to his feet, spraying bits of bone shavings everywhere. He grabs a stool from the far side of the room and moves it next to his spot, and then gestures that I should sit.

Oh. Is this explanation going to take a while? I hesitate.

Bek makes a frustrated sound and then points at the stool. "You are with kit. Be seated, or I will feel even more guilt."

"I'm perfectly capable of standing for longer than five minutes," I tell him, but I sit anyhow, and then add, "Thank you."

He returns to his seat, brushing aside bone flecks before crossing his legs again and picking up his carving knife. "I am trying to share, and you are not making this easy." When I say nothing to that surly statement, he adds, "I am not good at sharing."

No shit, Sherlock. But he's trying, so the least I can do is listen and not be mean about it. I don't want to be mean, anyhow. I just want to understand. "I'm here now. Go ahead."

I expect him to start carving again, but he pauses, looks thoughtful, and then glances up at me. "I feel guilt for how our pleasure-mating went."

Oh. That's not what I expected to hear. "It's in the past."

"It is in the past, true, but if I leave a thorn in my foot, it will still irritate and infect until it is removed."

Fair enough. "I don't think you should feel guilty. I just think we're two people that have very different personalities and don't know how to get along together. I don't dislike you. I actually like you a lot and wish we were friends." Saying all this feels so incredibly difficult. My shoulders are tense with worry, and I can feel the stress taking over my body, which is weird. It's like I just lock up around Bek because I expect him to disapprove of everything I say. I guess it's going to take a while for me to get over that, but I'd like to try. "I don't hate you."

"I do not hate you, either." He meets my gaze, and the look on his face is very serious. "I feel I treated you badly. I was not kind and loving like Ereven is to you. I was just...frustrated."

"We both were," I say softly. "It wasn't a good relationship."

"I wanted a mate very badly," Bek tells me in a low voice. "I have been alone for a very long time. I want a mate and kits. I thought being with you would give me that chance. But we did not have the bond that the others do. Resonance smooths the way when things are difficult, and we had no such thing to help us. I felt it was not right between us, too. It was not right, and the more I tried to hold you in place, the further away it felt you were moving. So I pushed harder and harder. I was not kind. And I lost you." He sighs heavily and gives me a tired look. "I think about why you left. I do not blame you for leaving me and ending our pleasure-mating. I was short and impatient, and you needed understanding, and you did not get that from me. But I do wonder if I had been a better mate to you, would you have still resonated to Ereven? If you had been happy with me, would your khui have pulled you elsewhere?" He shrugs. "I wonder about this."

I understand his frustration, but I'm glad that we broke up, because I have Ereven. Everything that was wrong with my relationship with Bek is right with Ereven. It's hard to explain or describe, but it just is. I can't say that to Bek, though, not when he is clearly still carrying feelings about how things ended between us. So I simply say, "I would like for us to be friends again."

"I miss you," Bek tells me.

I lick my dry lips and shake my head. "No, we are not doing this. I am happily mated."

His expression grows thunderous. "I know this. I do not seek to come between you. You resonated to another. You will never bear my kits. You belong to Ereven, and he belongs to you." He looks insulted that I would insinuate otherwise. "But it does not mean that I do not miss you."

"Do you really miss me?" I ask him. "Or do you miss what you thought we had? Are you lonely for me, or are you lonely for a mate, any mate?" I'm a little surprised I'm able to speak so forcefully to him. "Because I remember what we had, and it wasn't good. We were always unhappy with each other. I don't want to go back to that."

"I..." He frowns. "I suppose I am remembering the good times." He stares off into the distance and then gives me a rueful look. "We argued a lot."

"It wasn't arguing. You'd get mad, and I'd shut down. Arguing implies I showed spirit," I tell him. "Pretty sure I wimped out of every argument."

"You did," he says thoughtfully. "It was very annoying."

"I'll bet. Look, Bek...you're lonely. I understand." I smile at him to make my words easier. "But it doesn't mean that we were meant to be mates. We can be friends, but that is all I want."

He sighs heavily. "It is all I want, too. I just...I do not know why I did this. I am not trying to make you uncomfortable, Claire." His expression is honest as he crouches low next to me. "You have been working hard for the tribe, and you want to bring nothing but joy to the others. I wanted to bring joy to you."

He's painting a pretty saintly picture of me, and I don't think that's true. "I'm just trying to lighten the mood, that's all."

"And look at the way you have befriended Asha," he says. "You have a good heart. I thought you deserved a reward for being such a good human. So I made you gifts."

I feel weird at hearing that. Like befriending Asha was some onerous task I took on. "Can you stop making me gifts? Save all that generosity for Borran and the gifts you're supposed to give him."

The look on his face grows stubborn. "I can give you gifts if I wish. It is my way of saying I am sorry for any worry I caused you in the past." His gaze drops to my belly. "And the next gift is for your little one."

That big noodle. "You're going to make someone a fantastic mate someday."

"Just not you." He gives me a devilish look.

"Just not me," I agree with a laugh. It's weird, but I feel like I regained a friend just now, and it's nice.

14

ASHA

I do not sleep much that night. I worry that the metlaks will return and brave the fire and our scents and come after the kit. I worry that Hemalo will take a turn for the worse, despite it being a slight head wound. I worry the kit will wake hungry and need me. So I do not sleep. I tend the fire and watch Hemalo as he slumbers. I make more mashed roots for the little one and feed Shasak when it awakens. It does not cry like a sa-khui kit when hungry, which is odd, but when he looks up at me with big eyes and waves his fist?

To me, he is a kit. A small, hungry, needy kit.

Shasak wakes up just before dawn, and I have to clean his bedding and wipe him down. His fur gets filthy easily, and I see why metlaks smell so foul all the time. This one will not be as bad as his brethren, I decide, and when he is clean, I hug him close to my teats and rock him until he falls asleep again. The cave is quiet except for the crackling of fire, and it gives me much time to think. I think of the astounded look on Hemalo's face when I revealed Shasak to him. He did not know what to make of the tiny metlak. I chuckle quietly to myself, thinking of his reaction. It was not the instant love I felt. More...befuddlement. I imagine he thinks it is like Farli's pet, except worse. But this is different. The dvisti is an animal.

Shasak is...not sa-khui, not human, but a people all the same.

My khui begins to sing as Hemalo rolls over in the furs. His eyes are still tightly closed, but I can hear the gentle resonance coming from his chest. It ignites an ache in my body, and I have to fight the urge to crawl under the blankets with him and seek out his cock with my hand. Wake him up with a stroke of my fingers along the length of it, watch his eyes open sleepily to gaze at me with such hunger and lust that it steals the breath from my lungs. It is the resonance that makes me crave him, I tell myself. My heart is still wounded at the fact that he has abandoned me. He has not apologized for leaving me behind. He has not even seemed apologetic.

I cannot let my relief over his safety cloud my judgment. I followed him out into the snows because I wanted answers, and now he is here before me. I can get the answers I need. All I need to do is wake him up. I could lean over, kick him as he sleeps, and try to make him as angry and as hurt as I am. To let him know how it feels.

I do not, though. Instead, I watch him sleep, my heart aching and sad. I gaze at the bandages over his high brow, let my attention wander over the proud sweep of his horns, the pleasing length of his dark mane. The strong line of his jaw. His broad shoulders are hidden by the furs, but under them I know his stomach is hard with muscle, just like any hunter, and his cock is as large and pleasing as any. Even more pleasing to me, I decide, because he has very prominent ridges on his cock, and they slide into my cunt in the most perfect of ways...

I feel my cunt grow wet with arousal, and I sigh, pressing my thighs tight together. I want Hemalo, but I also want to know why he left me. I do not know if I can mate with him until I know the answer. Does he...not want me? I touch my mane and the ridges of my own jaw. Does he find the humans more attractive than a female of his own kind now that all of his tribesmates are mating them? Does my sa-khui nose bother him because it is not ridiculously small like a human one? Are my teats too flat compared to the puffy, fleshy ones of the humans? I glance down at my chest. It is a good chest, I think. My teats are large enough to feed a kit, but not so bouncy that they jiggle when I move, like Claire or Shorshie. I do not think I would like that very much.

But...perhaps Hemalo likes that? I hate that I am filled with so many questions. I should wake him and demand answers.

And yet...I am worried what those answers will be. What if he tells me things that wound my spirit and devastate me? I am terrified of what I might hear. What if it means we are to never be mated ever again? That we will only fulfill the call of resonance and then he will abandon me once more? What will happen to the kit we make between us? The worry gnaws at me until my belly aches with it, and I pick up Shasak and cradle him close to my chest, seeking comfort. Him, I do not mind waking up. Shasak is simple—he wants nothing more than to eat and sleep. I stroke his strange, furry face and fight down my scared feelings.

The fire flickers and begins to smoke, a sign that more fuel needs to be added. I pluck a dung chip out of a basket and add it to the base of the fire so it will smolder. I hold Shasak as I lean in over the fire, and as I do, I glance up at the entrance to the cave. I am not sure why I do, but when I look over, I see eyes shining in the slit between the cave wall and the privacy screen.

Something is watching me.

I get to my feet slowly, uneasy, and hold Shasak close. I know what is out there. I know whose eyes watch me from outside the cave but will not come in. The two metlaks that raided this cave and attacked my mate have come back. I feel a protective surge for Shasak—and a greater one for Hemalo. They will not hurt my mate again. I will not let them.

I keep my movements slow and creep over to the edge of the cave, where my belt hangs on a rock ledge. I pull my knife out of its sheath and clench it tight in my free hand. Let them come in.

Shasak chirps suddenly, and the sound is loud in the small cave. Hemalo stirs in his bed, and outside, I hear an answering chirp.

Hemalo's eyes open, and he looks at me.

"I know," I murmur softly, holding my knife high. "They have come for the kit." I am angry at the thought. They left him here alone, filthy and unguarded. They do not deserve to have a kit. I can take much better care of him than they ever can. He is mine now.

Hemalo sits up slowly. He gets to his feet and then puts a hand toward me. "Give me the knife. You have the kit. Protect him, and I will protect you."

I nod. In this, we will be a team. I hand him the knife and hold Shasak closer to me, stepping back to the rear of the cave. Hemalo stands before us, tall and strong despite the bandages on his brow, and for a moment I feel a stab of fear. If many metlaks wait on the other side of the privacy screen, he will need more than my small bone knife. "Be careful," I whisper.

"I will protect you," he tells me. "Do not worry." He grips the knife tightly and steps forward, then pushes aside the privacy screen.

I suck in a breath.

The screen clatters to the side, bouncing against the cave wall. The two metlaks out in the snow cringe back and hiss at us, one scurrying behind the other. The larger one, I can see, only has one eye. "These are the same metlaks as before," I tell Hemalo.

"Stay behind the fire," he warns me, and brandishes the knife at them. "Back!"

They drop back a few steps but then wait, hovering patiently in the snow. The smaller one lifts its head and chirps, and the kit in my arms answers. The smaller one chirps again and takes a step toward Hemalo. She crouches low to the ground, her body language that of groveling and submission. But her gaze is locked on me and the kit in my arms.

She wants him back. I clench Shasak tightly to me. She does not deserve him back. Not if she left him.

"They are so thin," Hemalo murmurs, shocked. "Is that why they came to the cave? Are they starving?"

"Does it matter?" I feel a sense of panic in my belly. Shasak is mine now. They do not deserve him.

Hemalo cocks his head to the side, studying the metlaks cringing at the entrance to the cave. "They are not leaving. They are terrified, but they do not want to leave. Odd."

"Chase them away. Make them go."

He glances back at me. "I do not think they are a threat. Remember what the human Li-lah said? They helped Rokan when he was injured. Do we have more roots left?"

I gasp. "I am saving them for Shasak. You cannot give them away."

"Be sensible, Asha," Hemalo says. He lowers the knife—but still keeps it out—and extends his hand to me. "Give me one of the roots, please."

"No!"

"Either they are people or they are not." He glances back at me, and there is reproach in his gaze. "Would you let Shasak's mother and father die? Right here? Right now? When they are clearly risking their lives to get him back?"

But I do not want to give him back. I fight down the helpless fear and frustration I am feeling. Hemalo is right, though; I cannot say that Shasak is a person and then let his kin starve like animals in the snow. I move to the back and dig through my pack, pulling out one of the few roots I have. I do not have many and will need to go hunting for more, and am feeling protective of my small store. I hand it over to Hemalo anyhow, though, because I know it is the right thing to do. I hate that it is, but I cannot be cruel.

He crouches low, his tail perfectly still, and offers the root. The one-eyed one races forward and snatches it, then bounds away. The smaller one remains, chirping and cringing. She is not interested in food. She wants her kit. Her gaze remains on me and the bundle in my arms.

"This must be the mother," Hemalo murmurs. "I think she is injured. Look at her arm."

I lean over to see around him, and the female cringes back a step. It is clear she is favoring one side. I feel a surge of guilt as I watch her move. She is not using one arm at all. Is this why she left little Shasak in the cave? Because she could not carry him but was desperate to find something to eat? What would I have done in her situation? "Should we give her more roots?"

Hemalo looks at the huddled female metlak and then back to me. "She wants her kit, Asha."

I feel like weeping. "He is happy with me. I can feed him."

"I know," my mate says simply. "But what would you do if someone took your kit?"

I think of my sweet Hashala, born so small and unhealthy. I would have fought anyone, done anything, climbed any mountain if it would have helped her. Hot tears spill from my eyes, and I hold Shasak closer. I do not want to give him up. I just want to love him and take care of him.

Shasak chirps.

The female echoes the chirp, edging forward another step. She reaches toward me with her good arm, and then draws back again, uncertain. She is brave, this female. She moves closer to the fire—and to the both of us—even though her mate has run off to eat. As she does, I see the fur on her bad arm is matted and filthy and crusted with blood. "We cannot send Shasak with her," I whisper to Hemalo. "She is injured."

"Then we must help her," he tells me gently.

I nod, even though I feel like screaming. Shasak is so warm and heavy in my arms, the perfect size. He is a good kit. I do not want to give him back. Yet as the mother metlak stares up at me with big, liquid eyes, I know I will not be able to keep him. "How do we do this?" I ask.

"Give me another root," Hemalo says, his gaze on the female.

I get another out of my bag and hand it to him. He offers it to the creature, but she only chirps and looks expectantly at me.

Even her hunger cannot sway her from her kit. I have an idea, and I crouch on the ground, holding Shasak out. "Here," I whisper. "Come see him."

She creeps toward me, chirping hesitantly. As she moves, I can see her ribs through her thick, matted fur, and my heart aches. Why are they so hungry? Did the earth-shake send them far from their home, too? "It is all right," I say in a low, soothing voice. "We are here to help."

The female reaches for Shasak, even as Hemalo gets to his feet and moves to the fire. He gets a length of leather and dips it into the water I have warming in the pouch, and then approaches the female, squatting next to her. She cringes back, hissing.

I hold Shasak out again.

She reaches for the kit, and Hemalo reaches for her arm again. The female hisses once more, but does not run away. She growls low in her throat and hisses, but her long hands creep toward Shasak, and she touches him, making sure he is all right.

"Do not let go of the kit," Hemalo murmurs to me as he begins to dab at the terrible wound on her arm. "If you hold him, I think she will stay long enough to let me help her."

I nod, and my gaze meets the mother metlak's. Does she understand that I am trying to help her? That I want nothing more than to love and care for her kit? Perhaps she does, because she does not snatch him from my grip. She strokes his fur and chirps at him, while Hemalo cleans the wound. Sometimes he hits a sore patch and she turns to hiss at him, but she does not move away.

"Is it broken?" I ask him as he continues to wash it.

"I do not know. I do not think they have a healer." He looks concerned.

A terrible thing. I have never thought about how precious Maylak is to our tribe—I have always harbored a little resentment for her because she did not save my Hashala. But how much worse would we be without a healer? She worked tirelessly to heal Pashov in the cave-in. She has watched carefully over the births of so many kits and fixed many wounds, all without complaint. To have no healer at all must be that much more dangerous. I wonder if the female and her mate have a tribe or if they are alone. Perhaps that is why they are starving. Perhaps her tribe died in the earth-shake.

"Her arm will need to be sewn," Hemalo murmurs to me. "The flesh is badly torn. Do you think she will sit still for that?"

I stare at him, aghast. "Who will do that? You?"

He shrugs. "I am good with an awl. Unless you wish to do it?"

I do not. Just the thought makes my stomach churn. "Will she sit still?"

"We will use intisar to numb it and hope she does not notice."

"And if she does?"

"You and I wear a few new scratches." He gives me a faint smile. "If we do not, though, her arm will not stay clean."

I nod slowly. "There is intisar in the baskets." It is one of the few plants that the metlak did not eat.

For the rest of the morning, we tend to the wounded female. It takes time to chew up the intisar roots and longer still to slather the wounded arm so it can be numbed. As Hemalo works, I make soothing sounds and stroke Shasak's furry head, and then stroke the female's head as if to suggest that we are friends, that I am taking care of her. I offer the root again, and she takes it, chewing frantically even as she touches the kit in my arms over and over again. She seems to feel that if she can touch her kit, that all is well. She hisses at Hemalo as he sews her arm, but otherwise ignores him. Occasionally I see a shadow pass in front of the cave entrance, and that tells me that the male is outside, waiting, but not brave enough to come inside. Hemalo is careful with the female metlak, taking care of her wounds as if she were his own, and stitching the flesh as tight as possible. He rubs more intisar paste on the wound when he is done and wraps the arm in a length of leather, tying it off at the wrist. The female hisses at him and immediately tries to chew on the ties. Hemalo adds more paste to the outside of the leather, giving me a rueful look. "If we make it taste bad, perhaps she will not be in such a hurry to eat it."

It seems to work; the female chews again and then makes a face, her tongue flicking over and over again as she tries to get rid of the numbing, foul intisar paste.

"What now?" I ask.

"Now," he says, and his voice is incredibly gentle, "we should give her her kit back."

My heart aches. I have to swallow the knot forming in my throat. "I do not want to. I want to keep him."

"I know. But would you want someone to keep your kit from you?"

I would not. I slowly hand him over, every bone in my body protesting. The female immediately snatches him from my grip with a surprising ferocity, hauling him against her chest. She scuttles backward, hissing at us one last time before racing out into the snow. I hear a couple of angry hoots and calls from her mate, and then they are both gone, leaving only their stink behind.

My heart feels as if it is breaking all over again. The cave is silent. The blanket I cradled Shasak in is empty in my arms. It should not hurt as much as it does, and yet I feel hollow and so alone all over again. I cannot stop the tears from falling down my cheeks.

"Asha, my mate," Hemalo murmurs, such tenderness in his voice. He comes to my side and puts his arm around my shoulders, pulling me close against him. "It is all right to be sad."

I sob against his shoulder, burying my face against his neck. I ignore the excited hum of my khui, because my heart hurts too much to think of such things right now. I think of Shasak, so small and trusting in my arms...and the way his mother snatched him back and raced away from the cave. All we tried to do was help her. Will she have enough milk to feed him? Will she discard him again to go hunting, and this time it will not be someplace safe because we are in their cave? My heart is full of worry and sadness, and I cannot stop weeping.

"Shh," Hemalo whispers against my mane. He strokes my back, over and over again. "I have you."

For some reason, that just makes me cry harder. He does not have me. He has left me. I only found him because I came after him. I cannot stop weeping. "Everything I love leaves me."

"I am here." His big hand rests on my lower back, and then he squeezes my side. "Feel me against you."

I shake my head, so sad that I feel it deep in my soul. "You left me, too. Always, you leave me."

"Is that what you think?" His big hand cups my jaw, and he forces me to look up into his eyes. There is such sadness there, sadness and love, and it makes me ache all over again. "You think I choose to leave you?"

I feel his tail trying to twine with mine, and I flick it away. I push at his shoulder. "What should I think? When I need you the most, you turn your back to me. Twice you have done it now! You left me after Hashala died, and you have left me again now that we resonate? Tell me what I am supposed to think of that." My voice grows in strength with anger and hurt.

He stares at me for a long, long time, saying nothing.

"What?" I say, feeling defensive.

Hemalo sighs. "I am a fool. I should have explained myself."

"That would be nice," I say tartly, though I do feel better to hear him call himself a fool. It is what I have called him in private, after all.

He brushes his knuckles over my cheek, and I want to start crying again at how good it feels to have that small, loving touch. "I left you because I care for you."

"That makes no sense," I tell him, pushing his hand away. "Only a fool would say such a thing."

"Perhaps so, but it was how I chose to help." The look in his eyes is so sad. "I left our mating because my presence made you angry. Every time you looked at me, you were full of fury. You attacked me with words, and you sought the furs of others. It made me feel like my presence at your side was making things worse. I thought maybe if you had time to yourself, time to heal, then you would come back to me." He gazes at me with such love that it feels as if he is touching my cheek all over again, even though his hand is not moving. "And even if you did not come back to me, if you were happy, I could live with that. It is your sadness that tears me apart."

I swallow hard. What he says is true. I was not a good mate. After Hashala died, I was numb. And then, I got angry. I lashed out at everyone, but most especially at him. If Hemalo said anything to me, I attacked. If he looked at me wrong, I spat ferocious words at him. I kicked him from my furs. I destroyed his leathers and his work when I was upset, which was often. "I was a terrible mate. But I felt you were not even trying to understand me."

"I was not," he agrees softly. "I was lost in my own grief. I wanted you to turn to me for comfort, and instead, you turned away and made me your enemy. I felt as if I lost both my kit and my mate in the same day."

That hurts. It hurts the most because he's not wrong. I did not think about his pain, only my own. The apology I want to say sticks in my mouth, though. It is hard for me to unbend, to accept that I have been the terrible one in this mating. That he was quietly trying to be there for me and I pushed him away. It does not make me feel good. So I tell him the only thing that comes to mind. "I never went to another's furs."

"If another male would make you happy, I would give you to him," Hemalo says gently. "I know you have never wanted to be with me."

I open my mouth to protest, but have I not said the very same words to him in anger? Before we mated, I enjoyed flitting from the furs of one male to another. I liked being coveted by every hunter in the tribe and choosing to bestow my favor. I never looked at Hemalo, because he was always quiet, never loud or demanding. He was content to stand in the background. When we resonated, the entire tribe was shocked, but no one more so than I. It was like I had seen him for the first time when my khui sang to his. At first, I was upset. Why did I not get one of the strong, brash hunters that flirted with me?

Why did I get the quiet tanner who was content to stand in the background?

But resonance chooses. And I think it chose wisely for me. Over time, I grew to appreciate that Hemalo was steady and quiet. I learned to like his soft smiles and gentle voice. I liked that he was content to let me shine while he stood behind me. We never competed for attention, he and I. Hemalo is happy to let me take the lead. I did not realize how pleasant it was and how right for me he was until I lost him. Everyone else in the tribe eventually irritates me with their words or their demands. Not Hemalo.

Perhaps I pushed so hard against him after Hashala died because he did not fight. Because he did not rage like me. He was quiet in his sorrow, because he is always quiet. Why am I just now seeing this? Why did it take me so long to recognize that because he is different than me in personality, he will grieve differently than me, too?

I feel ashamed. "I might not have picked you at first, but you are the only one I can see myself with. You are the one that is right for me...except that you keep leaving," I add, unable to resist jabbing at him. "Twice now you have abandoned me."

He gives me a small, rueful smile that makes my belly flutter. "It is because the throbbing here," he begins and presses my hand over his heart, "means that it makes the throbbing here," he says as he leads my hand to his cock, "unbearable."

"Do you think it's more bearable for me if you leave?" I retort, and stroke his cock through his leathers just to be spiteful. And maybe because I enjoy teasing him. Maybe. I feel a shiver move through my body as he hardens under my grip, and his khui begins to sing even louder. I cannot resist touching him, just like I cannot stop the wetness that creeps between my thighs.

"I thought of Jo-see, actually," Hemalo says.

That stops me cold. I lift my hand, frowning. "Jo-see?" That small, chattery human?

He nods. "Jo-see left and she was able to bear not mating to Haeden for almost a full turn of the moon. I thought perhaps if I left, it would give you time to adjust to the idea of being my mate again. That I could return when you were ready."

It is the sweetest—and most ridiculous—thing I have ever heard. "That is foolish."

He sighs and rubs his brow. "I seem to think many foolish things around you."

"This is true. Why did you not talk to me?"

"You think I do not wish to talk? I talk. It is you that does not wish to listen."

I scowl at him. "You never talk to me. You never tell me what you are thinking. You force me to guess, and I guess wrong. I would never tell you to leave our cave, and I would never tell you to walk away when we resonate! It solves nothing!"

"You never talk to me, either. You think it is easy for me to see you hurting and when I try to find out what is bothering you, you turn me away? You snarl at me and push me aside? You never tell me how you feel. I am your mate. Your happiness is everything to me. You think it does not wound my heart when you want nothing to do with me?"

I glare at him, but the tears come again, because I know he is right. I am not good at expressing myself when I get angry. I shut down and hide away. "I will try harder," I grit out, and it sounds very sullen, even to my own ears.

"All I want is for you to talk to me when you are troubled or when you are hurting."

"I am hurting right now," I say hoarsely, thinking of Shasak out in the cold with his dirty, hungry mother. More tears start to flow from my eyes, and I cannot help myself. My lower lip quivers, and then I bury my face against his neck again, because it is too much for me to handle.

"I know you are." He strokes my mane, his hands and voice soothing. "You are full of love and want a kit of your own. You want to be a mother."

"I am a mother. My kit is dead." I sob. "I still miss her."

"I miss her every day, too. That will not go away, Asha. But we can keep our memories of her and still move on with our lives. She would want you to live. She would want you to be happy." He strokes my cheek. "And you have not been happy."

I have not. Not since she breathed her last. I have been miserable and tried to make Hemalo miserable, too. "Sometimes I worry I do not know how to be happy."

"I think you do." His caresses feel wonderful against my skin, and he smells so good. I love huddling against him. For the first time in a long time, I feel warm and protected and strangely calm. I am crying and upset, but...I still feel it will all be all right. Is this what I have been missing? Hemalo's soothing love?

Perhaps I am a bigger fool than he is.

I sniff, snuggled against him. "I am still going to miss Hashala."

"I know."

"And now Shasak, too. He was mine, even if I only had him for a day." I barely had Hashala for longer.

"You can miss them both," he agrees. "But you cannot allow it to destroy your life."

He is right. Still, I think of Shasak and how small and helpless he was in my arms. His mother was starving and injured, and the one-eyed mate to her not much better. "What if they cannot survive the brutal season?" I whisper. "What if I have sent Shasak back with his mother just to starve to death?"

Hemalo pats my back, reassuring me like he would a kit. Once I would have found it irritating, but today I find it soothing. "If you wish, we can spend a few days gathering roots and bringing them back to the cave so they will have food to eat. We can see if they will follow us, since they know we have food. If they do, perhaps we can lead them somewhere where the food is more plentiful."

I suck in a breath. What he is suggesting, no other hunter would consider. Take time during the brutal season to feed metlaks? But Hemalo does not think like a hunter. He never has. "You would do such a thing?"

"Of course. You are my mate, and it is important to you." He rests his chin against the top of my head, next to my horns. "And for a day, he was my son, too."

Tears blur my eyes again. "You are a good mate. I am sorry I have been so awful to you."

"Not awful." He touches my cheek again. "Just unhappy. And I did not work harder to make you happy. I retreated into my own hurt, thinking I was doing what was best for you. I will talk to you from now on, I promise."

"And you will not leave?"

"Never," he whispers. His fingers graze my chin once more, and then he tilts my face up. We gaze at each other for a long moment, and then he leans in and presses his mouth to mine.

I draw back, surprised. "What are you doing?"

"A mouth-mating, like the humans do." He looks puzzled. "Did I do it wrong?"

"I...do not know." I press my fingers to my lips, curious. My khui is singing loudly, but I do not know if it is because we are snuggled close or because the mouth-mating is exciting.

His smile is gentle. "Then we will have to practice it."

15

HEMALO

Six Days Later

"Are they still following us?" Asha murmurs as she moves to my side, wading through the deep snow. "Or did we lose them?"

I glance backward, squinting at the distant ridgeline. My eyes are better than hers, and I can pick out the yellowish coats of the metlak in the distance, even against the endless white hills. "They are still there."

"Good," she says, her expression brightening. "I think this is a good valley. Lots of plants. They will have plenty to eat here."

I grunt agreement, turning forward again and wading through the snow. The weather has been foul off and on, dumping snow every time the clouds appear. Between storms, Asha and I have been collecting roots to feed the metlak couple. We leave them outside of the cave every evening, and by morning they are snatched away again. It does not matter how much food we put out, either. It is all gone by the morning. Asha frets that they do not know how to pace themselves, to save food when their bellies are full. She worries what will happen if we leave.

I do not want her upset, so we stay on, even though I wish to return to the tribe. I will not leave without her...and my need is a selfish one, I admit to myself. I want to take her back to the vee-lage so I can claim her as my mate. So she has no more distractions. I force myself to be patient, because I know this is important to her, and she is important to me.

So we hunt roots every day for the metlaks. Trudging through the thick snow and digging out roots takes its toll on both of us, and by the time we return to the cave each night, we are both exhausted. The days that the weather is bad, we have kept to the cave. I thought perhaps it would be awkward between us to be alone again, but we have fallen into an easy companionship once more. Asha keeps busy with weaving and cleaning, and I work on scraping furs. We chat, and she tells me about Claire's plans for the haw-lee-deh that we are missing. I suppose we should be upset about not being with the tribe for the celebration, but I am enjoying the quiet time with my mate. It's nice to be alone with her, just the two of us. When we return to the vee-lage, I will give her the presents I have been holding back, waiting for the right time to give her. To show her that my love is unchanging.

But until then, I will be patient and let Asha take the lead.

We walk, and my khui hums in my chest as her hand grazes my arm. My cock immediately hardens, and I reach through my layers of clothing and tighten my loincloth against my flesh. It is difficult to walk with a stiff cock, but I cannot stop. Nor do I want to call Asha's attention to the fact that I am full of hunger for her. I am letting her lead in this, as well. She will call me to her side when she is ready to mate. Until then, I will endure silently...

...and take myself in hand whenever I have a quiet moment to myself.

I hear Asha's khui singing to mine, and it makes me smile even as my body fills with tension and need. Perhaps it affects her differently than me. Sometimes, I can smell the scent of her arousal in the air, but she has not indicated that she wishes to mate. She ignores resonance and ignores the song in her chest, so I suspect it does not fill her with the aching, bitter need that I feel. Perhaps she does not wake up in the night, full of unfulfilled desire and hunger. If this is true, then it is good. I do not like the thought of Asha suffering.

I will gladly pay whatever I must to ensure that my mate is content, and if that means ignoring my cock as if it is a frozen, useless limb, then that is what I will do. Until then, I will just imagine spreading my favorite fur cloak onto the snow and laying her down upon it. I will think about pulling off her thick, woolly leggings and revealing her long, beautiful blue limbs and the smooth, bare cunt that seeps with arousal. I will dream of burying my face between her legs and licking her until—

"Do you think they will follow us into the valley?" Asha asks, interrupting my thoughts. "I would hate to think we have come all this way for nothing."

"They will follow," I reassure her. "Do not worry." And I force myself to think of metlaks again, instead of my mate's sweet limbs or the way she sighs and clutches at my horns when my tongue is buried deep inside her.

"I just want to be sure they are well off before we leave them," she frets. "We cannot stay out here forever."

I am glad we are agreed on that. "They follow us yet," I reassure her, extending my tail backward to her. I am pleased when her tail twines with mine in response. Just a brief touch, and then she detangles it once more, but it is enough.

Today, we have decided that since the metlaks cannot be trusted not to eat all of the supplies we gather them, we must bring them to the food. So we have gone out, trekking through the snows despite the bone-deep cold. Metlaks are territorial and do not venture far in search of food. I believe these two will starve before leaving their territory...but they also know we have food and provide things to eat. Our hope is that if we find a good place with many plants, they will realize that food is nearby and move someplace new. At least, that is our hope. I secretly worry the metlaks might be too stupid to realize this and will continue to follow us endlessly, all the way back to the gorge that houses the vee-lage.

"There," Asha murmurs, pointing ahead. "I see a cluster of chadok roots. They like those."

"And there is a stream in the distance," I agree, noting the puffs of steam rising from the thread of blue at the far end of the valley. I pause and look back at her, walking close behind me. "This is a good place. Perhaps we should dig up a few roots and leave them in our trails?"

She bites her lip, her small fangs white against her mouth. "I do not know if that is a good idea. What if they continue to think we are feeding them? Perhaps we should just make sure our trail goes past the plants and let them figure out the rest."

I nod agreement. What she says is wise.

We spend the afternoon walking around the valley, pausing by each cluster of plants. There is a variety of foliage here, enough to feed several families of metlaks throughout several seasons.

Asha is encouraged when she looks back and sees the metlaks stopping by a few plants to dig them up. By the time the suns begin to lower in the sky, we have trekked around the valley several times and paused by every bit of greenery in the hopes they will realize what we are trying to show them. My mate begins to slow down, her steps lagging as the day goes on. She is tired, but when I suggest we return to the cave, she refuses.

"We have to make sure they have food to eat," she tells me, protesting.

"We have led them past food several times today," I say, patient. "They know how to eat, or they would not have grown to adulthood. Let them be, Asha. It will grow colder by the hour, and we must return to the cave so we do not freeze."

"But," she begins, and then sighs, flinging her arms up. "Fine! We will return to the cave." She stomps away in the trail I have cut into the snow for her.

She knows I am right, and so I do not get mad at her frustration. Asha has always burned hot. I move to walk next to her, keeping pace with her angry storming. She ignores my tail when I caress hers, a sign that she is angry, as are her hunched shoulders and deadly silence.

I let her sulk for a bit, and then when she continues to remain quiet, I decide to prod her. "Asha."

"What?" Her tone is sullen.

"Are you angry? We promised we would tell each other if we were upset, remember?" It is one of the many good conversations we have had in the last two hands of days. One of our big problems is not talking to each other, so we have agreed that if we are upset, we will tell the other. It is a good rule, but we have not had to put it to use...until now. In the past, I would let Asha bluster all she wanted, assuming she would get it out of her system. However, I am learning that her anger is a cue for me to pay attention. That when she is wounded, she turns thorny because she is hurting and she needs to be distracted away from the hurt. So I will make sure she does not dwell on it. "Talk to me."

"Yes, I am angry," she snaps back, casting an irritated look over her shoulder at me. "Is it not obvious?"

"Tell me why."

"Because I am not ready to leave yet!"

"Because you are not ready to abandon the metlaks and their kit, you mean?" I press.

The look she sends me is full of anger. I lift a challenging brow. She sighs, and her lower lip trembles. "I just...what if they cannot take care of Shasak?"

"If they cannot," I say, keeping my voice low and soothing as I move forward and put my hand on her back, "then there is nothing you can do to change the situation. They are metlaks. They are wild creatures. Let them be. If we were not here, they would find their own food. We must let them survive as they must."

"I still worry!"

"Of course you worry. They will not be as good parents as you and I." She looks surprised at my response, and I add, "But they are still his parents."

She sighs heavily. "I think I liked it better when we did not talk."

"No, you did not," I say easily.

"No, I did not," she agrees. "I am just being prickly."

"You are." I brush my tail against hers and am pleased when hers twines with mine. "But I would not have you any other way."

Her smile is faint, but it is there. She reaches for me and puts her hand in mine, a human sign of affection that makes my heart leap with gladness. "I just want to know they will be all right."

I pat the pouch at my hip. "I saved a root from our walk today. We will leave it outside the cave. If they take it, we will know they followed us back instead of staying in the valley. If that is what happens, then we will lead them to it again tomorrow. We will not let them starve, my mate."

Her eyes shine with relief, and she squeezes my fingers.

I WAKE up in the middle of the night. It is so cold that my tail—sticking out from under the furs—feels numb. I tuck it in and gaze up at the ceiling, sleepy. I am exhausted, but Asha is pressed against me, her hand on my side, her cheek tucked against my shoulder, and it is making my khui sing to hers. My cock aches painfully, and my entire body is brimming with unfulfilled need. She slumbers on, though, so I do not wake her. I slide out from her grip and stretch, moving to the entrance of the cave. I step outside, shuddering at the intense cold, and relieve myself quickly. The root we left out is still there, iced over. That means the metlaks stayed in the valley. Good. Asha will be relieved. I move back inside, replacing the privacy screen over the entrance, and head to the fire to stoke it up.

Asha sighs in her sleep, turning. I glance over at her absently, and then go still. She is on her back, and the blankets have slipped. Her tunic has hiked up, revealing one teat, the nipple erect. I close my eyes, because a male can only be so strong. My khui sings forcefully, demanding that I get back into bed with her. If I do, though, I will surely touch her...and I do not want to push her into mating with me again. I want her to want me.

But it is cold outside of the furs, and her body is so warm and inviting. I hesitate, and then move back to the bed. I grasp the hem of her tunic to pull it down over her tantalizing body. Even as I do, a wave of her arousal perfumes the air, and I realize her hand is between her thighs, cupping her cunt. I can smell the slick heat of her.

It is too much.

I bite back a groan and move under the blankets, pushing her thighs apart. She makes a small noise, stirring, but does not fight when I press my mouth to the mound of her cunt. Instead, she moans, breathless, and spreads her legs wider. I cannot tell if she is awake or asleep, but her body wants mine. I bury my mouth in her slick folds, dragging my tongue over their sweetness. She is soft here, soft and perfect, and I groan with the taste of her on my lips. I must have her.

Asha moans, and her hands go to my horns, like they have in the past. She pushes my face down, toward the entrance of her body. I obey her, letting my tongue glide down her slick cunt folds until it dips into her heat. She is fiercely hot here, hot and slick with need, and I lap up the taste of her. "Hemalo," my mate breathes, and the sound of my name on her lips nearly makes me spend my seed. I groan and drag my tongue over the entrance to her core, then thrust inside her with it. She cries out and arches against me, and I mate her with my mouth, pushing into her cunt with my tongue over and over again, as I know she likes. I use one arm to brace my body on the blankets, and with my other, I grip her at the base of her tail.

She makes a high-pitched, keening noise, her legs jerking against my shoulders, I can feel her hands tighten on my horns, and her breath puffs out rapidly. "Yes," she pants. "Yes! My mate!"

I growl with pleasure at the sound of that. I know how to touch her, how to make her body sing like her khui does. I know everything she likes, and it feels as if I have been given a gift to be able to touch her once more. I do not care about the need throbbing in my cock. I do not care about myself. There is only my mate, Asha, who must be pleasured. I want to make her come, want to taste the juices that will flow when her body clenches up and she screams out her release. She is so wet right now, so full of need that I cannot stop pumping my tongue into her sweetness, lapping it up and pleasuring her at the same time. She whimpers, the sound sweet and agonizing all at once.

I grip the base of her tail tighter, and she squirms in my arms, wild. I cannot use my tongue fast enough, so I decide to use my hand, as well. I lick her folds as my fingers push into her sheath, and use my hand as I would my cock, thrusting into her with my fingers, until she is crying out my name once more and her juices flood onto my hand. I enjoy her shudders, leisurely licking her clean as she comes down from her pleasure, until she pushes my face away and collapses on the furs.

"I was not sure if I was dreaming," Asha murmurs as I lick my way up her belly to her hard, perfect little teats. I cannot resist tasting the nipples, just once.

"Not a dream," I tell her, my voice raspy with need. "Just your mate desperate for a taste of you."

She gives a dreamy sigh and traces her fingers along the length of one of my horns. "Shall I do the same for you?"

I shake my head and drag my tongue over one of her hard nipples, then roll back onto the furs. "No."

"No?" She sits up and rests on an elbow, looking at me in surprise. "You do not want my touch?"

I want her touch. I want it more than anything. But I want it freely given, not as thanks for my pleasuring her. "It is late, and you are tired. Rest."

She is quiet in the dark, and then prods my arm with a finger. "I thought we were supposed to talk to each other."

I chuckle, because Asha knows me better than anyone else. "Fair enough. I want your touch, but I want it too much. If you put a hand on me, I will throw you down on these furs and thrust into your cunt until dawn."

She shivers. "And this is a bad thing?"

"I want it to be because you want it freely, not because I have licked you and made you feel good." I pause and then look over at her. "I want it to be your idea. It does not mean the same if it is something I have convinced you to do."

Asha nods slowly. "I understand, I think. And for me to touch you right now would not be the same, would it?"

It would be pleasurable, but it would not be what my spirit craves. I want my mate back at my side in every way. I want her heart and her body to be with me, not just her body. I swallow back my raging need and nod.

"Very well." She curls up against my side again and pulls the blankets over us. A yawn escapes her, and she is quiet for a long time. I lie in the darkness, gazing at the embers of the fire and trying to ignore the pulsing throb of my cock. Asha is quiet for so long that I am convinced she has drifted off to sleep. But then, she speaks. "So I am to pounce you, it seems. A surprise pouncing."

I chuckle. "I suppose so. But it has to be something you want." I squeeze her shoulder, hugging her tight against me. "If you are not ready, I am content to wait."

Most of me, anyhow.

16

ASHA

The metlaks have not come back, so there is no reason for us to stay in the cave much longer. Part of me is sad to see the root uneaten in the morning. It means that they will either feed themselves...or starve to death. Hemalo is right, though. I cannot care for a family of metlaks, not when food is so precious to the sa-khui in the brutal season. I miss the warm, fuzzy bundle of Shasak, though, and my heart aches at the thought of him going hungry. I will always worry, I suppose. Hemalo says there is nothing wrong with that, and I agree. It is just who I am. I want to take care of a kit, any kit, given to me.

I am not completely focused on metlaks this frosty morning, though. There is no snow falling this morning, but the skies look gloomy and dark, and we will stay put until it clears once more and then head back to the vee-lage. Hemalo, ever busy, finds things to do around the cave. He has already sharpened his weapons, packed his bag, and is now scraping the skin of a snowcat pulled from the nearby cache. I repaired a hole in one of my boots, but as the morning wears on, I find myself bored. I pick up a basket of dried leaves to sort into tea flavors, but my mind is not focused. It is quiet, and I find myself unable to sit still for long. It is not just the concern over Shasak and his family. It is my own unfulfilled resonance and my relationship with my mate that my mind keeps focusing on.

Last night, I was restless in my sleep, and he comforted me with his mouth. I had not realized how much the resonance was affecting me until he put his tongue on my skin, and then I was full of need. I loved every moment of it, and it felt so right to be together again. It felt...good. Perfect. But then he did not want me to touch him in return, and it hurt. I am glad he told me his reason, but I am still fretting about it this morning. His words were not unkind, but I still feel rejected.

And that is why I do not move to him right now and demand that he mate with me. Because deep down, I still worry he will reject me like he has in the past. That I will do something wrong and he will leave me once more. I know it is a silly fear, and he has reassured me, but I cannot help it. I need to be less afraid before I can move forward.

I gaze down at the basket between my legs, frowning.

"What troubles you?" Hemalo asks, not looking up from the skin he is scraping.

The words I want to say stick in my throat. "It is nothing."

"A lie," he says calmly. "Not even a good one."

I hate that he is right. The truth will not budge from my mouth, though, so I cast about for something else to tell him, anything that will distract him. My gaze focuses on his mouth, the soft, fascinating line of it. "Mouth-mating," I blurt out. "Kissing."

That gets his attention. He stiffens and glances over at me, the look in his eyes full of heat. "What of it?"

"What made you decide to try it?"

He gazes at me for so long that I feel my khui begin to hum in response. "The hunters seem to enjoy it with their human mates."

He speaks the truth. Every time I turn around, it seems that a human is putting her mouth on her mate. It is not a sa-khui custom, but that does not mean it is bad. It just seems very... intimate. I toss the idea around in my mind and then say, bravely, "I should like to try it again."

"The mouth-mating?"

I nod. I feel very skittish. If he turns me down, I do not know what I will do. The humans always look so glad to be mouth-mating. But what if Hemalo is not feeling very 'mouthy' at the moment? What if—

"Let us try," he says quickly, interrupting my worried thoughts. He puts aside the skin he is working on and rinses his hands in the small bowl of meltwater he keeps at his side. The flutter of excitement in my belly grows as he moves to sit next to me, and when I remain still, he reaches out and takes the basket gently out of my lap. "Shall we move this?"

"Of course." I feel silly. I have mated with this male before. I have borne his kit. A mouth-mating is nothing. But for some reason, it seems very important.

He puts the basket aside and then takes my hand in his. His grip is warm, dry. Mine feels clammy, and my palms are sweaty. I am so nervous. Why am I nervous? "Would you like for me to mouth-mate to you, or do you want to mouth-mate to me?"

"Does it matter?"

"I only ask because if we both move in at the same time, we might scrape each other's lips." He puts the tip of one finger on his fang and grins at me.

Ah. He has a point. The humans do not have to worry about such things, because they have weird, square little teeth. "I will take the lead, then."

He nods and waits.

I lean in and put my hands on both sides of his face, just in case he moves around. I do not want to do this wrong. I lean in and push my mouth against his, waiting. It feels...unexciting. I frown and meet his eyes. "What did you think?"

"I think they do it with open mouths."

Oh. I guess I have not paid close enough attention. Usually when the mated couples get affectionate, I turn away. "Open mouths, you say?"

He gives me a slow nod. "Like my mouth on your cunt. It is more like licking each other, I believe."

I feel a flush of heat through my body at the reminder of what we did last night. Lick his mouth like he did my cunt, eh? I study his face again, strategizing, and then lean in and mash my lips against his again, then push my tongue forward, into his mouth.

A wave of heat immediately pulses through my body. I gasp against him, because the shock of my tongue moving into the hot well of his mouth is...stunning. He groans, pulling me against him, and his hands go to my buttocks, dragging me into his lap. "Again," he murmurs against my mouth.

I want to do it again, too. I go with my instincts, licking gently at the seam of his lips, and when he opens for me, I flick inside, exploring. My cunt is throbbing and wet, and I am incredibly aware of the press of his big body against mine. I cradle his face as I lick at his mouth, and when his tongue moves against mine, dragging lightly, it feels as if his tongue is moving along other, more sensitive parts of my body.

Oh.

Oh, I see why humans do this.

"I think I like mouth-mating," I whisper between darts of my tongue. I cannot get enough of this. I like the position, too. I am straddling Hemalo's lap, with his hands on my backside. His tail flicks against mine, and I automatically let mine wrap around his, locking us together. My hands move over his cheeks, and I bury them into the thick length of his glossy mane, deepening the kiss. I am tired of soft, playful licks. I want deep, hungry licks like he does to me when he is trying to make me come. So I drag my tongue deep into his mouth, and thrust, mimicking mating.

His groan of response makes me breathless. He holds me tighter, and the kiss gets deeper, our tongues playing back and forth as we toy with control. Sometimes he takes the lead, mouth-mating me with hard, sure thrusts that make me ache between my thighs. Then I decide I want control again and fist his mane as I delicately sweep my tongue along his.

By the time we break the kiss, we are both panting with need, and the scent of my arousal is heavy in the air.

"I like that," Hemalo rasps, his eyes hooded with desire. "I enjoy mouth-mating very much."

"I do, too," I murmur. My khui is singing to his so loudly that it feels as if it is trying to drown out the sounds of our own voices. Hemalo gazes up at me, pure need on his face. I know if I tell him to mate with me now, he will push me onto my back and be inside me before I can draw another breath.

The thought is exciting...and frightening, as well. What happens after that? Do I raise our kit alone? Are we mated? I need more from him before I can move forward. Last night when he pleasured me, it was good, but I am still confused. "Can we stop there?" I whisper. "I need to think."

He leans in and presses his mouth to mine in a light caress. No hungry thrusting of tongues. Just a nuzzle of his lips to mine. "Of course."

"Thank you." I slide off his lap and detangle my tail from his, and I feel sad that I do not wish to continue. A mating is nothing but two bodies joining together for pleasure. It should be nothing to fret over.

But this one feels important. This next time we come together, it has to be just right.

The air between us feels thick with tension, and we pass the rest of the day in a restless sort of calm. We talk, we laugh, and we work, but there is something that makes both of us unsettled. My cunt feels hot and needy, and I want to push my hand—or his face—between my thighs and relieve the tension, but that feels like it is something I should not do. Not until my mind is settled.

The root outside is still undisturbed. The metlaks have not returned, and when the suns come up in the morning, I am sad to see that the weather is pleasant and the skies clear. That means that I must say goodbye to Shasak for good. I know he is already gone, but part of me hoped I would find them outside the cave, waiting, and the mother would hand her kit back over to me. It is just a dream, I suppose. It still makes my heart sad.

Hemalo seems to sense my grief. He is full of caresses and comforting touches this morning as we dress in layers and strap on our packs. He gives me a deep, searching kiss before we leave the cave, and I am so breathless and distracted from his mouth that I forget all about being sad when he takes my hand and we walk away, heading back toward the vee-lage.

Travel during the brutal season grows tiring fast. I have a new appreciation for what the hunters go through day in and day out while I sit in the vee-lage, cozy near a fire. The air is so cold that each breath burns, and every bit of skin exposed to the air feels numb. The snow is deeper than I have ever seen, and Hemalo quickly takes the lead so his larger body can forge a path for me to walk in behind him. I grow cranky with fatigue, and I want to chastise him for leaving the tribe—and me—behind. But every time I open my mouth to complain, I see a mental image of him, prone in the snow, the metlaks standing over him. And I swallow back my anger. The travel is miserable, but we are both safe.

Because the snows are high, though, our travel is slow, and by the time the light starts to fade in the sky, we are nowhere close to the protection of a hunter cave. Hemalo is not worried, though. He finds us a sheltered spot near a rock bluff, and we both gather extra fuel to burn throughout the night. We make a fire and put our backs to the rock, and between the two, it is not so bad. I still shiver despite my furs, and so Hemalo pulls me into his arms, and we huddle together near the fire's warmth.

We do not talk, but it does not matter. Hemalo's presence at my back is comforting, and his body heat keeps the worst of the cold away. My eyelids grow heavy with sleep, and I am just about to drift off when his tail brushes against mine. It is an intimate touch, and it fills me immediately with longing. I think of the kisses we shared yesterday and how I was too afraid to go further.

And then I think of Hemalo, on the ground, with the metlaks standing over him. Every moment we have suddenly seems precious. I clutch his hand, pressed over my shoulder. "Hemalo?"

"Mm?" He sounds drowsy.

"You know how you said it would be my choice to decide when I touched you again?"

"I remember." His khui begins to sing, telling me that he is suddenly very aware of me.

"I wanted to yesterday."

He chuckles, and the sound is low and delicious, his voice moving over me like a rippling blanket. "I wanted to yesterday as well. Why did you stop?"

I hold his hand tightly to my chest, anchoring him against me. "I am afraid." The words squeeze out of my throat, half-choked. It is so difficult to speak them, to bare myself to him and hope he will understand. That he will not abandon me a third time.

To my surprise, Hemalo nuzzles against my throat, his mouth warm as he presses it against my skin. "I am afraid, too."

That is not what I expected him to say. "Why are you afraid?"

"The same reasons you are, I imagine. I worry you will hate me and we will struggle again. I worry about the kit we will make. I worry if anything happens to it, it will destroy what we have again." He kisses my cheek. "But I do know that I am more afraid of not trying."

I want to cry, because I know just what he means. "I have lost a kit and survived. But I do not think I can survive if I lose you again. Please, never leave me again. Not because you think it's good for me or because it is what is needed—it's not. I need you at my side. I need you with me, supporting me, no matter how dark things get."

He nods slowly, and his fingers tighten against mine. "I was a fool to leave before. I thought I was helping, but I see now I have only made it worse."

"You did," I reply, trying to make my response light and teasing. "But I forgive you."

"You forgive me?" He presses another kiss to my neck. "Then I am the luckiest of males to have such an understanding mate."

"You are." I slide his hand to my teat, resting over my nipple. My entire body is aching for him, and my khui is singing so loudly it feels as if it is going to echo off of the rock cliffs nearby. "If you swear you will never leave me again, I want to be yours. Now. Tonight."

"Tonight? In this cold?"

"There are parts of you that are very, very warm," I say encouragingly. "Your warm parts could give my warm parts a greeting."

"While I would like nothing more," he murmurs into my ear, his tongue flicking against my lobe, "I do not like the thought of a metlak chancing upon us while mating."

I smile. He has a point.

"I want to wait until we return to our howse back in the vee-lage," he continues. "I want to take you home so we can start our family again. So we can do this right." His hand slides from my teat down to the waist of my leggings and pushes inside. He cups my cunt, his fingers stroking through my slick folds. I moan as he pushes a finger inside me and continues to nuzzle my throat. "I want you in my furs every night for the rest of our lives. Even when you are angry at me."

I cling to him, gasping. "I want that, too."

"I want a howse with you. I do not want to live with the hunters, and I do not want you to live with Farli. You belong with me." His finger pumps inside me, as quick and desperate as I feel. "In my furs. Taking my cock. Bearing my kits."

A shudder of pure pleasure rocks through me. I want all that, too. "Yes," I breathe.

"You will not share a howse with Farli. You will come to my bed, and you will wrap your tail to mine and spread your legs for me, because you are my mate."

"Always."

"Tell me that you are mine, Asha," he growls into my ear, and then nips the edge of it with his sharp teeth. I cry out, because my body is so sensitive that even that small action sends me into an avalanche of pleasure. My cunt clenches around his finger, and then I am coming hard, the air leaving my lungs as he continues to whisper in my ear about how I belong to him.

It is the most erotic thing he has ever told me, and I savor every moment of it.

17

CLAIRE

Days Later
Ugly Gift Day

It is the last day of the holiday celebrations. The poison clumps hung in the lodge are starting to wilt, and the decorations are looking tired, but everyone in the tribe has been having a wonderful time. I cannot stop smiling at the group gathered near the fire. Lila and Maddie are leading the 'White Elephant' gift exchange. It's a name that means nothing to the sa-khui, so we've taken to calling it the 'Ugly Gift Day.' Each tribesmate was instructed to bring a hideous present to give to the others, and as the game goes along, people laugh with sheer joy at the silliness of it.

Lila gestures at Rukh, who is holding a basket and looking as if it is going to bite him. His mate, Harlow, holds their baby and has a broad smile on her face. Lila indicates that Rukh should open, but he gestures back to her. They're too far away for me to make out their hand signals, but I can guess what it is. Something like "Heck no." He eyes the presents around the circle of tribesmates—a bag of terrible tea leaves, a stained tunic, a pair of leggings with one cuff sewn shut—and eventually trades his basket for the neatly wrapped stack of dung chips that Zolaya is holding. "Fuel," he says, shoving his basket into Zolaya's hands. Everyone roars with laughter, and Georgie is wiping tears of mirth from her eyes. Zolaya pulls the lid off the basket, peers inside, and immediately makes a face. "Dirty loincloths!"

People crack up, Maddie signs it to Lila, who is waiting patiently, and then the sisters laugh, too. It's cute. I love that everyone's having so much fun. Even my Ereven is by the fire, waiting his turn. His basket has an egg in it—a good gift for a human, a terrible one for a sa-khui. He catches my gaze and smiles at me. I wave from afar, content to stand on the sidelines and let the others lead things. It's been a long holiday event, and while it's been a lot of fun and taken people's minds off of the brutal season, I'm ready for a break. I don't mind organizing, but I don't like being the center of attention. Maddie has no such qualms and is hamming it up as the circle moves to the next person, Harlow. Maddie does sign language and talks at the same time so everyone can hear what she has to say, and she's playing the role of announcer beautifully.

"You are not playing?" A person comes and stands next to me at the far end of the longhouse.

I know the voice, and I turn and smile at Bek, rubbing a hand on my rounded belly. "No, I got the fun of setting everything up. I get to watch everyone else play. Plus, I don't really feel the need for dirty loincloths or a shoe with no mate." I smile, watching Farli hold up her shoe and offer it to Harlow.

"I have one last gift for you," Bek says. "I know you do not want it, but it would honor me if you would choose to take it anyhow." He extends a small, leather-wrapped package to me.

"Oh, Bek. Please don't." My smile becomes strained. "Truly. I don't want any gifts." I'm still thinking about our awkward conversation the other day, when he told me he missed me. I was hoping we'd landed at friendship, but him arriving with another gift while I'm by myself makes me worry. Has he not given up on me?

"It is for your kit. Take it." He pushes it toward me.

My kit? Reluctantly, I take the package and untie the string. Inside the wrapping is a beautiful baby blanket, pure white and the perfect size for a half-human, half-sa-khui baby. The edges have been carefully stitched, and the entire thing is whisper-soft. "It's lovely. Thank you."

"I am happy for you and Ereven," Bek says quietly. "I may not always show it, but all I have ever wanted is your happiness. You are a good person and you deserve happiness."

I smile at him, but I'm troubled by his words, even after he moves away. It seems to be a recurring theme that I've heard a few times as the holidays rolled onward and Asha hasn't been around. Everyone thinks I'm a saint because I've befriended her. Or that being friends with my ex will suddenly make me a better person.

It's crap.

I must be frowning, because Ereven gets up from the gift-giving and comes to my side, standing where Bek was not a few moments ago. "What is it, my heart?"

"It's nothing. Really. I'm just in a bad mood."

"Would you like to go for a walk?"

I gesture at the group by the fire. "You'll miss the last holiday event. Are you sure?"

"I would rather spend the time with my mate." He smiles at me and offers me his arm, something he has learned after a discussion of human courtship rituals.

I link my elbow in his and show him the blanket. "Bek gave us a present for our kit."

"That is kind of him. He is a good male."

There is that 'good' word again. Why does someone have to be good or bad? Why can't they just 'be'? I frown as we leave and head down the main street in Croatoan. The laughter in the longhouse trails after us, at odds with my thoughts. Asha has missed all of this, and I wanted her to get some of the credit for all of the work we put in. Instead, everyone seems to think I did it all by myself and somehow 'took on' the burden of Asha to boot.

"You are very unhappy," Ereven says, wonderingly. "What is causing my sweet Claire to glower so?"

"Just something Bek mentioned." I bite it back, but it keeps gnawing at me. "The tribe keeps going on and on about how I'm being such a good friend to Asha and taking the time to befriend her, and it bothers me. They act like it's such a big chore to be her friend, but Asha's never been anything but helpful and kind to me."

"To you," my mate agrees. "Do not forget that she has been unpleasant to many of the other human females since they arrived. They are allowed to feel differently about her."

He's not wrong, but it feels disloyal to even think it. "It's just that...she worked hard on the holiday celebrations, too, and she hasn't been here to see any of them. She hasn't gotten any of the credit, and she hasn't gotten to see any of the fun."

"If she resonated to Hemalo again, I imagine they are having their own kind of fun," Ereven teases.

"Ha ha," I say glumly. "I just worry about her. They've been gone a while."

"You want everyone to see her for the person she is, not the person she has been," Ereven says, pausing to brush a lock of hair off my face. "You have a kind heart, my Claire."

"Oh stop—"

"You can have a kind heart and it does not mean that Asha was difficult to befriend. They can be two separate things." He taps my cheek with a finger. "It does not mean anything at all, except that perhaps your example showed people that they should have tried harder to pull Asha from her shell. They are grateful, because not only did they have a good holiday, but they will have an old tribesmate back. Asha is more like herself now than ever, and you are a big part of that."

"I guess." I still think Asha is the only one to take the credit for Asha's recovery, but any way you look at it, I'm glad the tribe no longer tiptoes around the whole 'Asha' topic. Everyone does seem to be excited for her and Hemalo to come back. "I'm just a worrywart."

"I do not know what that is."

"It means I won't be happy without someone or something to fuss over," I tell him, squeezing his arm tight as we walk. "You might get the brunt of it for the next few days."

"I will gladly take the brunt of your attentions," Ereven says, and he makes it sound filthy and funny at the same time. "But until then, can I show you my present for you?"

I stop in my tracks, my jaw dropping. "You didn't!"

His eyes twinkle with devilish delight. "I did."

"But, Ereven, babe, we talked about this! We said we weren't doing gifts."

He leans in and touches his nose to mine. "I lied, my Claire."

"Oooh, you're the worst."

"Do you want to see it?"

"Well, I'm curious now," I grumble, but I can't stop smiling. I'll have to make it up to him...in a lot of different ways. He's going to be in for a few sexy surprises over the next few weeks, I think. What a sweet man. I have no idea why Bek's presents feel awkward but I'm tickled at Ereven's thoughtfulness. I suppose because I know Ereven's heart, and Bek is still a mystery to me.

Ereven is grinning with excitement as he leads me to one of the abandoned huts in the back of the village. It's one that no one ever goes to and is used for storage—or so I thought. Inside, there's a baby crib. It's very much a Not-Hoth crib, made of carved bone instead of wood. The rockers on the bottom are two sa-kohtsk ribs, and the inside of the cradle is a leather sling and lots of furry white blankets. It's a complicated, thoughtful present, and Ereven must have had one of the other humans sketch out to him what a crib was, because it looks just like a human one. "It's so amazing. How..."

"Many, many hours," he says. "Many hours imagining your smile when you see it."

"It's so much work," I tell him, awed. The crib is put together with dozens of bones, and each one is smoothed out and carved to perfection. "But how—"

"Bek helped me."

I turn to him, shocked. "He did?"

He nods. "He wanted me to know there were no hard feelings. He wishes to be your friend again—and mine. I think he has finally moved on."

His expression is tentative as he looks at the crib and then back at me. "Do you like it?"

I turn and fling my arms around his neck. "I love it!" I press a kiss to his face. "And I love you. So much."

As I move to the side of the crib and run my hand over the smooth railing along one side, I think about all the gifts I've been given—every single one unasked for. Maybe I've been interpreting the giving spirit wrong. All I've wanted to do with organizing the holiday was bring a little bit of joy to the monotony of the brutal season and to make people smile. To give them something to look forward to.

Maybe that's all Bek wanted to do for me. Make me smile. Give me something to look forward to. He helped my Ereven make me a crib, wanting nothing more than to brighten my day.

It's the thought that counts, and I feel like I have the most thoughtful mate—and the most thoughtful friend in Bek—out there.

I can't wait to show this to Asha.

18

ASHA

Days Later

"I see the gorge," Hemalo calls over his shoulder. "We are almost home."

After days of travel in the ice and cold, I am relieved. The thought of my warm, snug howse with its stone walls, cozy fire, and my thick furs is enough to make me beam with pleasure. I have enjoyed the time with him, though. It has brought us closer together and taught us to communicate. We have no one else to talk to as we journey, and so it forces us to speak to each other, even when he is prone to be silent and I am likely to be annoyed. To my surprise, speaking to Hemalo balances my mood, and I find that I can pull what is bothering him out of him with a mere question. It is like we are learning to be mated all over again.

The travel has been so slow—and so cold—that we have not had a chance to pursue our resonance. By the time we stop most nights, we are both so tired and half-frozen that even khui-induced mating does not appeal. Our khuis have been mostly silent—perhaps realizing our bodies are too tired—but there is a low hum of energy inside me at all times. It seems to be rising the closer we get to the vee-lage, and I watch him as we walk. I am fascinated by the way his shoulders move as he strides, and the slow, steady flick of his tail. Though most of his body is covered with thick furs, I spend a lot of time mentally pulling those furs off and admiring him. Underneath his leggings, his buttocks would be taut and deep blue, thighs thick with muscles. His hands under his protective mitts are big and strong, and I love the lines of his back. Dreamily, I imagine yanking off his tunic and finding him completely naked underneath.

It would be impractical in this weather, of course, but so nice to have all that skin suddenly exposed to me.

As we near the gorge, Hemalo moves faster, his steps quicker. He is refreshed with energy now that our goal is in sight. As we get closer, however, my relief gives way to nervousness. How will the tribe react to our return? We have both missed all the days of the haw-lee-deh, and it is sure to be mentioned. Repeatedly. What if they tease us about leaving?

Worse, what if someone says something to pull us apart just as we are coming together again? We have been together on the trails, out in the wild, and been happy. What if that changes now that we are about to be around the others again? Nervous, I flick my tail forward, brushing against his. He immediately twines his with mine, a comforting gesture.

I feel better. A little, anyhow.

"All right?" He calls back over his shoulder, glancing at me.

"Just my mind full of bad thoughts," I tell him. It is still hard to tell him what I am thinking without getting defensive, but I am trying. The old Asha would have pushed aside his concerns and made a hurtful comment.

"It will be all right," he reassures me. The old Hemalo would have been silent. "Nothing they say is meant to hurt. They are our tribe. They want us to be happy." He pauses and turns around, reaching for me. He takes my gloved hands in his, concern on his face. "What troubles you so?"

I shake my head. "It is...difficult to explain." His hands holding mine helps, though. "I feel...as if the tribe does not understand me sometimes. When I grieved, I felt as if they did not grasp why it took me so long to get through it. Why everything would make me sad and why I would hide away. I felt like they wanted me to act like I was not suffering, and that made it hurt even more." I lick my lips and blurt out my biggest worry. "What if we return and everything goes back to how it was?"

"Impossible," Hemalo tells me in that rich, comforting voice of his.

"How is it impossible?" I can see myself falling into the bleakness all too easily.

"Because I will be at your side every moment of every day. When you frown, I will give you mouth-matings until you smile again. When you are sad, I will hold you close until you are happy again. When we sleep, it will be together, under the same furs."

I sigh, because what he says sounds so nice. "Do you promise?"

"I do. You are my heart, Asha. Nothing comes before you. Do you understand?"

I nod slowly and move forward into his arms, tucking myself against him. "I still do not feel ready to see everyone again. Not just yet. I wish we could race to a howse and just put the screen over the entrance and not come out until we are ready."

He chuckles and strokes my cheek with his glove. "My heart, we can do exactly that."

I look up at him in surprise. "Really?" My Hemalo is more social than I am. He loves to be around the tribe and talk around the fire. I am the one that pulls away first, the one that would be content to be at home at my own small fire instead of surrounded by others. I have been anticipating our return as hour upon endless hour of tribal celebrations, stories shared, and people feeding us and fussing over us until we can slip away. And while it sounds nice, it also sounds exhausting. Hemalo would enjoy every minute of it, but I would much rather retreat to my furs until I am ready to face them. I am pleased to hear he wants the same thing. "Are you sure?"

"If it is what you want, it is what I want. The others can wait to celebrate." He rubs my back. "We can boot Farli from your howse, light a fire, and relax until we are ready to emerge."

I pull a glove off, then reach down and caress the base of his tail where it emerges from his leathers. "It might be a while before I feel like seeing the others." When I hear him suck in a breath, I tighten my grip. A sa-khui tail is sensitive at the base, where it joins the skin, and Hemalo is more sensitive there than most. I wonder, idly, if the humans have figured this out...and what they have figured out that I do not know. Perhaps I should ask Claire sometime. I let my fingers trail along the underside of his tail. "When I have you alone, I might feel...very un-social."

"All the more encouraging," he says, a husky note in his voice. "Does this mean you are ready to fulfill resonance, Asha?"

"I…am still a little scared."

"Of losing the kit?"

A knot forms in my throat. "What if we lose it again? What if we break again?"

"We will not let it break us again." He leans down and brushes his nose against mine in an almost-kiss that feels somehow more intimate than mouth-mating. "Look at how far we have come. We are talking, are we not? We say the things we hid before. And I miss Hashala. I will still miss her. But I have room in my heart for more."

I do, too. So many more. It is the wanting them so badly that terrifies me. What if I want and it never happens? Am I doomed to hold only the kits of others and never my own? I give him a panicked look.

"Stop," Hemalo murmurs, shaking his head at me. "You are worrying too much. Whatever happens, we will face it together. Let the world bring what it does. I will take it all on as long as I have the perfect mate at my side."

His words fill me with warmth. I give a playful snort. "You have a strange idea of perfect."

"No, I do not." He smiles. "My perfect is a tall, strong female with lovely blue skin and a generous, giving heart. A female with fire in her heart to spare."

The knot forms in my throat again because he makes me feel so good. How did we grow so far apart before? "You are my heart, Hemalo," I whisper. "Let us never be bad to each other again."

"Never." He nuzzles my nose and then presses his lips to mine. "We will fight from time to time, but we must remember that we are better together than apart."

I drag a finger along the underside of his tail again. "I want us together. More than anything."

He growls low in his throat. "Female, I am close to throwing you down in this snow and claiming you right here."

My body tingles with excitement, and I feel a surge of answering heat between my thighs. "What is so bad about that?"

"The fact that other hunters might come upon us mating in the snow? Or the fact that I have had more snow in my backside in the last hand of days than I would care to?"

I laugh, because he always knows how to bring my mood back from the brink. "Then let us go find my howse and kick Farli out."

He grins at me, surprisingly boyish, and then grabs my hand. "Come, let us hurry."

We race forward—as much as one can race in the thick snows—and when we get to the edge of the gorge, we both hurry down the rope ladder with great speed. At the bottom of the gorge, it immediately feels warmer out of the wind, and my face feels flushed. Perhaps it is because I am thinking about mating.

A great, great deal of mating.

We race through the canyon, heading for the vee-lage. The snow is nonexistent down here, and we can run as fast as we please. It seems like it only takes moments before the rock path turns to neat stones and the vee-lage comes into sight. In the distance, I see people walking between howses, and two humans are talking in front of the long-howse. Curls of smoke rise from several teepees, and I catch sight of a familiar human with a rounded pregnant belly as she walks with Tee-fah-ni, both of them carrying baskets full of dirtbeak nests. Claire sees me as well and raises a hand in greeting, her face lighting up.

I pause, wondering if I should stop and speak to her.

"There is no smoke coming from your howse," my mate reminds me. He takes my hand and gives it a squeeze. "Unless you have changed your mind?"

I look over at him, at the simple love and understanding on his face. He is the best of males, my mate. "Oh, I have not changed my mind," I tell him with a grin. I grab the front of his tunic and pull him toward my howse on the outskirts of the vee-lage. I glance over at Claire, and she has a hand to her mouth, hiding her laughter. She understands.

There is no explaining what needs to be done. I feel light and free, and I laugh as I drag my mate into my howse. Farli is not inside, and the fire is cold. Good. We are to have our time alone, and this makes me happy. I pull Hemalo inside and then push the privacy screen over the entrance, shutting us away from the world.

"Do you need a fire?" Hemalo asks, moving toward the fire pit. He shrugs off his pack and glances over at me.

I do not need anything but him. I grab him by the front of his tunic again and press my mouth to his in a quick, fierce kiss.

He groans, forgetting all about the fire, and his hands go to my face. He cups my cheeks, and our kiss grows deeper, more passionate. My khui begins to sing loudly, and his chest vibrates with a strong, urgent song. This feels good and right. I lick at his mouth, frantic for my mate. My tongue slicks along his, teasing and coaxing in a playful manner. My kiss is light and teasing, but the urgency in my body is anything but. Our khuis demand a mating, and they will get one.

I jerk at his leathers even as we kiss, tugging him toward my bed and the furs there. "I want you," I tell him. "I want this. I want us. I want our kit."

"I want all of that," Hemalo says thickly. "I have waited forever to hear you say those words to me, my heart."

I smile at him and undo the knots that hold his heavy overtunic closed. We are wearing so many layers it is frustrating to pull them off. I want my mate naked, his skin against mine. "So many clothes," I mock-growl.

"Would it go faster if I took them off?" he asks.

It might, but that would deprive me of the joy of stripping him bare. I shake my head and tear at his leathers with determination. Off comes the outer layer. Off comes the furry vest. Off comes his leather tunic, and then his delicious, broad chest is bared to me. I make a noise of satisfaction, skimming my hands over his skin. How long has it been since I touched him? I want to put my mouth everywhere. I want to lick him in all of his warmest, softest spots and make him shiver. I love the power that I hold over him, and the intensity in his gaze as he watches me. I press my hands over his heart, where the protective plates are thickest, and I can feel his khui singing to mine. "I love this," I tell him softly. "I did not dream it would happen for us again."

"May it happen a dozen more times," he whispers. "I will be glad of every one."

I will, too. I kiss him again, mating my tongue to his, and I can feel my thighs quiver in response when the ridges of his tongue drag along mine. I undo the cords of his outer leggings, and then the ties of his inner ones. Instead of pushing them down his legs, I reach in and caress his thick cock, the head slick with thick, milky pre-cum. Hemalo groans into my mouth, shuddering at my touch. His hands go to my shoulders, and he holds me tight against him.

I stroke my hand along his length as I kiss him, and when my tongue plays along the length of his, I let my fingers glide up and down his shaft, then tease over his spur.

"This seems unfair," Hemalo tells me between kisses. "You are covered in furs and yet you are able to put your hands all over me."

"I am an unfair female," I tease back, sliding my hand to the back of his leggings and dragging my finger under the base of his tail again. He shivers, and I grin. "What are you going to do about it?"

He gives me a challenging look, and then his hands go to the front of my outer tunic. He puts his hands on the knots, and then, to my surprise, rips the leather asunder. It falls off my body and pools on the floor, and he goes to work on my next layer, ripping and tearing at it. I gasp, though I do not stop him —this wild, fierce side of my calm mate is making my cunt pool with heat. "My leathers!"

"It is good for you that I am a tanner, then," he rasps, and jerks the belt off of my tunic. Before he can rip it away, I pull it over my head. His hands go to my leggings, and he tears at them like a wild creature. I have never seen Hemalo this obsessed before. It is fascinating—and incredibly arousing. He drops to his knees before me and drags my leggings down my thighs, pressing his mouth to every bit of skin he can as he does so. I feel his tongue flick against my belly, my hip, my inner thigh... my cunt.

And I cannot help the gasp that escapes me.

"You are so wet," he whispers against my thighs. "I can taste your juices dripping down your legs, my mate."

"It is because my mate knows just where to touch me," I tell him. I caress his horn and then run my fingers through his mane as he presses more kisses against the bare mound of my cunt. "Though he is taking far too long to undress me."

He gives a mock-growl and picks me up by my legs, dragging me over to my bedding. His clothing is falling around his legs as well, and we stumble into the furs, falling together. He kicks at his leggings, and I do the same, because I want to be naked and feel his flesh against mine.

Then he surges forward, and the length of his body presses over mine, and I can feel all of him, from the hands that move to my mane, to the feet that brush against my own. His tail twines with mine, and I feel his knee nudge my thigh. I part my legs gladly for him and give a breathless sigh of pleasure when he settles his weight between my legs, his cock resting against my cunt. It is the most perfect feeling.

"My mate," Hemalo murmurs as he kisses me. "My sweet Asha. I would wait forever for you."

His words make my eyes prick with tears. "I do not want to wait any longer. I want...everything."

"Then let me give it to you." He kisses me again, resting his weight on his elbows. I feel his body shift and then the press of his cock against the entrance to my core. I raise my hips, encouraging him to enter me. To make me his.

He sinks deep in one swift movement that leaves both of us gasping. I can feel the thick length of him inside me, rubbing against the walls of my womb. His spur is nestled between my slick folds, coated with my juices, and the heat of him is breathtaking. It is perfect, the way he fits me. I did not realize how much I missed this until now, how full and complete I feel with him inside me. I give a sigh of pleasure and dig my nails into his shoulders. "This is where you belong."

Hemalo growls a response, and then I feel his body begin to move over mine. His cock drags inside me, and I moan at the sensations that even the smallest of movements gives. He thrusts deep, and it sends another wave of pleasure through me. Instinctively, I raise my hips as he pumps into me again, and the sensations double in their intensity.

I cling to him, whimpering. "My mate."

"Yours." He begins to rock into me, harder and faster, our bodies focused on an insistent rhythm. "My fierce Asha. All yours."

He is the fierce one right now, though, his body moving over mine with possessive heat that takes my breath away. I cannot keep up with his movements, my toes curling in response to the pleasure spiraling through me. It is too much to take, too fast, and the vibrations of my khui through my body as it sings only intensifies things. A gentle wave of pleasure crests through me, quickly followed by a harder, fiercer one. I cry out, and my mate only hammers into me harder, a look of grim determination on his face.

I am gasping, lost in endless pleasure as I come. I reach up to his face and caress it. "Give me your seed. Let us be whole again."

Hemalo shudders atop me and then surges hard and deep, body quaking. His release bathes my insides, a liquid warmth that pulses through me and leaves behind an intense feeling of satisfaction. I hold him against me, enjoying the mindless, endless pleasure that moves through my system. It seems to go on forever, and I love it. I do not mind even when my mate collapses on top of me, his cock throbbing deep within me. I wrap my legs around his hips, anchoring him to me. I want him to stay here forever. I am not done with him. Not in the slightest. It is going to be many, many hours—days, even—before I let him up from these furs.

"My Hemalo," I sigh happily, stroking his sweaty mane back from his face.

He presses another kiss to my mouth and then nuzzles my nose. "You are pleased?"

"More than pleased," I tell him, and then pat his flank. "Though I hope you have saved some of your strength, because I am going to want more."

A chuckle escapes him. "My mate is insatiable."

"Your mate, and her khui," I agree, feeling it sing in my chest. It is not silent yet. It will need more time to end its song, and that pleases me. "It wants us to mate more."

"It is just as demanding as you," Hemalo teases.

My smile fades as a sobering idea hits me. "We are going to make another kit by the time resonance is fulfilled." I tighten my arms around him. "Oh, Hemalo, the thought brings me such joy and such terror."

"It brings me nothing but joy," he murmurs, caressing my cheek before letting his hand slide down to one of my teats. He grazes my hard nipple, teasing the peak of it. "You will be a wonderful mother to our kit."

"I still think of Hashala," I admit to him. "And I still want her. Is that terrible?"

"It is normal," he reassures me. "You will never stop wanting her. But I imagine she would have wanted a sister...or a brother."

I like to imagine that, too. I smile softly at him. "How do you always know what to say to bring me out of my worry?"

There is a smile in his eyes as he leans forward and presses another tender kiss to my mouth. "Because I know you better than anyone. You are my heart, and I am yours. We will always be there for each other."

He says it, and I want to remind him of the past, when we have split apart so badly. But this time, it feels different. It feels... weighty, and real, like when Rokan predicts the changes in the weather. And I think, maybe, that Hemalo is right about this. We struggled in the past, but now we are stronger than ever. As long as we are together, we can take anything.

I slide my hand to his tail and grip the base, giving it a squeeze. "How is your cock, my fierce tanner?"

He groans and buries his face against my neck. "Stirring already."

Mmm. I smile.

19

ASHA

Three Days Later

When I wake up on a chilly morning three days later, Hemalo has his head resting on my teats and his tail is wrapped around my leg, anchoring me to him. I slide my arms around him, enjoying the feel of my mate in my arms...until I notice my stomach rumbling with hunger. Strange. It has not been noticeable since I resonated, because the singing of my khui to Hemalo has drowned out all other urges.

Curious, I think of my mate and wait for my khui to begin its loud song, but there is only a gentle, sated thrumming.

That means...

I press a hand between our bodies, touching my flat stomach. Inside me is our kit. Three brutal seasons from now, I will be holding my own little one. I am both filled with wonder and utterly terrified at the same time. I close my eyes and hope that this one turns out healthy and strong. If it does not...

Hemalo's arms tighten around me in his sleep, as if he can sense my thoughts.

If this little one does not turn out healthy and strong, we will grieve, but we will get through it together, I realize. I will not shut myself away from my mate with my sadness. I will tell him all of the hurt and anger I hold, and he will understand it and help me get better. I feel calmer with that realization, and slide out of the blankets. Hemalo sleeps on, even after I crawl out of bed. He is exhausted, my mate. We have spent the better part of the last several days in a mating frenzy, and between matings, napped and held each other as we talked. I am...starving. Starving and cold. Our fire has burned down to coals, and I put on a tunic and leggings, and shove my feet into my boots before heading to the fire to stoke it. We are out of fuel, though, and we are also out of dried meat. There is nothing to eat and nothing to burn. I should be annoyed, but I feel too good. I will just have to go out and get more supplies, then.

I glance back at my sleeping mate and then pull a fur blanket over my shoulders, pushing the privacy screen aside and peering out into the vee-lage. Things seem quiet, which means it is early, but I do not mind that. In truth, I need only fuel...and perhaps the sight of one particular person. I am brimming with the need to tell someone about what has happened, someone other than my mate.

As if my thoughts have summoned her, Claire appears out of her howse, a bundle in her arms. She pauses in the road and glances down at my howse. I step out of the doorway and wave at her.

Her round, human face brightens, and a big smile creases her face. She heads toward me, waddling as fast as she can with her burden perched over her belly. "Asha!"

I put a finger to my lips, pulling my privacy screen back over the entrance of my howse, then move out to meet her. I am surprised—and pleased—when she puts her arms around me in a hug. It is amusing to think this small human is trying to hug me, and I wrap my longer arms around her and hug her back.

"I'm so glad to see you've returned," Claire gushes, pitching her voice low as she glances around. "Everyone is wondering how things are going. You two have been so quiet in your house." Her cheeks turn a bright red. "Well, not so quiet, but you know what I mean."

I laugh. "We finally stopped resonating," I tell her, and put a hand to my stomach. Mine is completely flat, and hers is rounded like a ball, but I feel like we are united at this moment. "This morning, I think."

Her face lights up, and she gives a happy squeal, dropping her bundle as she flings her arms around me, hugging me all over again. Her joy just highlights my own joy, and I am laughing and crying all at once as she gushes about how excited she is for me. I am excited for me, too. For the first time in a long time.

She takes my hands and squeezes them, her gaze searching my face. "And you're happy? How are things with you and Hemalo?"

"We are good," I reassure her.

"Did you tear him a new one?"

"A new one what?" I ask.

"Human expression. Did you yell at him for leaving you behind?"

I shake my head. "It is a long story, better told around a fire." My stomach growls again. "Hopefully with food."

"Oh! I am the worst friend." She shakes her head and then puts a hand on her belly, leaning over to pick up her bundle. "I was going to leave this on your porch in case you guys didn't want to emerge just yet. I know when Ereven and I first resonated, it was hard to leave the bed for at least a week." The red is back in her cheeks as she holds the bundle out to me.

I take it from her, touched at her thoughtfulness. Unwrapping it, I can see that it is a package of dried meats, some roots, and another bundle of dung chips for fire fuel. "You are a good friend, Claire."

She waves a hand in the air. "Please. I'm just the first one to head over. You're going to be inundated with well-wishers once people find out you've emerged. Everyone is so excited for you both. Well, everyone except Farli," she amends with a small smile. "She wasn't too happy to be kicked out of her own house, but she understands. She's been staying with us until a roof is made for another one of the houses."

"I will have to make it up to Farli," I promise.

"Come. Do you want to go sit in the main lodge, or do you want to come visit by my fire?" Claire asks, putting her arm around my waist as if she is not the size of a kit and heavily pregnant. "I can feed you if you are hungry. Or do you want to return to your mate?"

I consider this. I do want to return to Hemalo, but the thought of talking to Claire is both soothing and fills me with excitement. I can tell her what happened and hear her opinions, and she can tell me what I have missed in the vee-lage while we were gone. And Hemalo will probably be asleep for a few hours yet… "Do you have something to eat at your howse?"

"Eggs," she says triumphantly.

I struggle to keep the smile on my face. Well, it is the brutal season and I cannot be picky.

She erupts in laughter at my expression, then shakes her head. "I'm teasing. I have stew from last night, and I just laid out some fresh red meat I was going to smoke. Ereven and Farli are both out hunting, so it'd be just you and me."

"Fresh meat sounds good," I tell her, tucking the bundle under my arm. "So how did the haw-lee-deh go? Did you enjoy yourself?"

She makes a face. "Did I tell you I found out who my secret gift-giver was? It was Bek! He was trying to apologize to me. It's sweet, but it still made me feel awkward." She sighs. "We are working on being friends again, but I still feel like I have to give him a gift as a thank you."

"You will think of something," I reassure her. Claire is one of the most thoughtful people I have ever met. She will come up with the perfect present to make Bek happy. I think about my mate, sprawled in my furs, asleep. "I did not make a present for Hemalo. I wish I had something to give him."

Claire pushes the screen away from her door and leads me into her cozy little howse. The fire is flickering in the pit, and it is warm and comfy in here. "Can you make him furs? Cook him something?"

"I am poor at both." I sit by the fire as she heads to her counter along the stone wall and begins to chop something. "But I want to make him happy. To show him I care."

Claire brings a small plate over to me, bits of fresh, juicy meat piled atop it. She sprinkles tea into her water pouch and then gives me a thoughtful look. "You could always blow his mind… do something surprising in the furs."

I lean in, curious to hear what human tricks she can share. The mouth-mating is fun, and I would not mind learning more. "Like what?"

She shrugs, sitting on a stool next to me. "This is going to sound personal, but it depends on what he likes. Is he into blow jobs? I know Ereven had never heard of them when we got together, so I don't think it's a sa-khui thing."

I tilt my head. "A below jab?" It sounds painful and not erotic. "Where 'below' would I jab him?"

"Blow job," she corrects. She pats my knee. "Girl, let me tell you all about it, then."

A SHORT TIME LATER, I leave Claire's howse with my bundle of fuel and dried meat, and my head spinning with ideas. We chatted for a while and I ate, and it was so nice to have a friend to talk to. I feel like my world is becoming slowly more complete. I have my mate, I am carrying another kit, and I have a good friend in Claire. I have a perfect little howse, and the tribe is full of kits and happy families. There is food—even if much of it is eggs—and I think of Shasak and his family and hope they are doing well in the plant-filled valley.

When I return to my howse, it is cold inside and Hemalo is on his back, snoring in the furs. I rebuild the fire and peel my leathers off, then slip back into bed with my mate. Instead of curling up against him, though, I begin to press kisses down his chest. Claire's instructions on blow jobs are so simple, yet so foreign to me. Hemalo has put his mouth on my cunt many, many times and pleasured me, yet I have never reciprocated. It has never occurred to me that it is something that is done. Of course, now that I have been told, I cannot wait to try it.

Hemalo groans in his sleep, his hand going to my mane and stroking it as I lick at his navel. "Do you wish to mate, my Asha?" he asks sleepily.

"Soon," I tell him, and continue to lick lower. "Right now I am giving you a present."

"A present?" He sucks in a breath when I flick my tongue over his spur. "What is it you are doing?"

"I am going to pleasure you with my mouth," I tell him, gripping the length of his cock in my hand and then licking the tip of it. The taste of him is salty and musky, but fascinating. Why have I not done this sooner? I watch him shudder when my tongue touches his skin, and I feel a sense of intense power and arousal at his response. "Do you want me to stop?"

"Never stop," he murmurs. His hand tightens in my mane.

I chuckle and let my mouth explore his length, my lips tracing along the ridges of his cock, exploring his spur, and testing out what things he likes. My fingers stroke his sac as I drag my tongue along the length of him. He sucks in a ragged breath, and when I lightly suck on the tip of his cock, he jerks his hips, as if trying to mate my mouth. I am intrigued by this reaction and take him deeper into my mouth.

"Asha," he rasps. "I might spill my seed. I am close. This is...too much."

I lift my mouth off of him and give him a smile. "Then you spill it in my mouth and let me taste you, like you have tasted me so many times."

His heavy groan tells me he likes that idea very much. I wrap my hand around the base of his cock again and take him in my mouth once more and begin to pump, like if my mouth was my cunt. I imagine him thrusting into me and try to mimic the action. Within moments, I feel his body shuddering, and then he hisses out my name. Hot liquid spills into my mouth, and then I am drinking him down as he comes.

When he is done, I give him a few moments to recover and drink some water to wash the taste from my mouth. It was not unpleasant, but definitely unusual. I am going to have to do that again many times in the future, just to enjoy Hemalo's reaction. I smile to myself and crawl back into bed with him.

My mate pulls me against him, tucking my body against his. "That was...the best present I have ever been given."

I chuckle.

"Next time, I should come in your cunt," he tells me, stroking my cheek. "So we can help resonance along."

"I do not think we have to worry about that any longer," I say softly. I take his hand and put it on my chest, over my heart. "My khui is no longer singing as loud. Do you feel it?"

"I...did not realize." There is a look of wonder on his face. "Then, we are to be parents once more?" At my nod, he pulls me close and nuzzles me. "That is the best present you could give me, my heart."

I smile happily and realize for the first time, there is no fear in my heart about this kit. We will take whatever happens, and we will love, no matter what. If we only have a handful of days with our next kit, we will make sure they are the best, happiest days ever.

And then we will hold on to each other.

EPILOGUE

ASHA

Three years later

"You lie," Maylak says, a frown on her face as she stares at Claire. Then she looks over at me. "Asha, she lies, does she not?"

I shake my head, groaning as I squat over the birthing mats. Both the healer and my friend are here to distract me as I give birth. My long pregnancy has been a calm one, but as the birth nears, I have grown more nervous with every passing day. My kit has bounced around inside me, reminding me that it is well, but I cannot be calmed. I think of Hashala and all the things that could go wrong. Even my poor Hemalo has been beside himself with worry. Ereven has taken him hunting for the day, just to get him out of the howse so I can strain over the birthing without him hovering over me. "She does not lie," I tell Maylak as another ripple moves through my belly, and the urge to push grows stronger.

"Truly!" Maylak's mouth drops open.

"It's true," Claire says, chuckling. "I swear to god, humans do that. Mouth on dick. I mean, you can put your mouth other places, too, but that's the most popular one. Ereven didn't like it when I sent my mouth exploring. He likes it one spot, and one spot alone."

"Where else would you put your mouth?" I ask Claire, curious. Another ripple moves over my belly and I hiss, because this one is stronger than the last.

Claire's face turns bright red. She gets up clumsily from her seat and offers the kit in her arms to the little girl sitting next to Maylak. "Esha, will you take Erevair to Georgie's house? I think Asha's baby is coming very soon."

Esha gets to her feet, all long blue legs and spindly arms, just like her mother was at that age. She reminds me of Maylak, growing up, and I think again how competitive I always was with the quiet healer. She has been a good friend throughout my long pregnancy, and strangely enough, I feel we are closer than ever. Esha takes Erevair from Claire's arms, hugs the kit close, and then gives me a small smile as she leaves.

"Let me feel your belly," Maylak says, moving to my side. Claire is heavily pregnant with her second kit, but Maylak is lean and thin, and I am envious of her compact body. I feel like a bloated, fat quill-beast. Her hand presses on my stomach, and then she nods. "The kit is ready to come out. You can push at any time."

"I am going to push anyhow," I snap at her. "Everything inside me is trying to push its way out."

Claire just giggles.

"And you," I tell her balefully. "What is it you licked that your mate did not like?"

Her laughter chokes in her throat, and she starts talking about human foods, of all things. As she babbles about something called a sah-lad, another ripple contracts over my belly and I groan, because everything is hurting and needs to come out. The tension in my body feels like a cord pulled to its breaking point.

"Keep going," Maylak murmurs in my ear, her hand on my shoulder. "Another push and we should see the head."

I am suddenly full of anxiety. What if my kit is too small to accept a khui? What if it does not live for long outside the womb again? What if—

Another spasm takes over my body, and I scream, bearing down hard. Maylak voices encouragement, and Claire moves to my side, ready with the birthing blankets to catch my kit.

"There he is," Maylak says, and I strain again. Then everything seems to happen at once, and I feel the heavy weight of the kit slide from my body. Claire catches him neatly with the blankets and cleans his mouth out as I pant, dizzy. The cord is cut, and both females move quickly.

"Is he well?" I ask. He is silent. So silent. Is he moving? Breathing?

Claire gives the tiny blue foot a little tap, and then an angry cry splits the air. My kit howls furiously, his lungs strong. I laugh happily, tears streaking down my face. He is just as outraged as can be, my kit. Claire cleans him off and hands him to me as I sit back on the furs, exhausted. "It is a girl," Claire tells me gently.

Oh.

I take my kit—my daughter—into my arms, and I cannot stop weeping. She is beautiful, this angry little girl. Her body is fat and healthy, and her fists wave angrily in the air as if she is furious at the cold. Her skin is a deep, healthy blue, and she has her father's proud nose and a tuft of thick black mane crowning her head.

"She is perfect," Maylak says, pride in her voice. "Very strong. She will have no trouble with a khui."

No, she will not, this one. I think of Hashala, and how small and weak she was. This daughter is just as beautiful, but the strength in her makes my heart ache with joy, and a little pang of sadness for what my Hashala did not have. I nuzzle my daughter close, my emotions choking me too much for words. I am filled with such love and hope. I weep happily as the angry little one grips my finger in her tiny ones, her face scrunched up furiously as she bleats about how much she dislikes the world she now finds herself in. It is not so bad, I think to her. I will make it good for you. And wait until you meet your father. You will love him. He will spoil you so.

"Do you have milk?" Maylak asks, her hand still on my shoulder as she sends her healing through me.

I nod. I do. I open the front of my tunic and tuck the kit against my teat. She roots against my nipple and then latches on, and the tears flow again.

I do not stop weeping even as my body expels the afterbirth, or as the females help me clean up. I cry through sips of tea, and I eat between sniffles. I ache and am sore, and I am also happier than I have ever been. My daughter is perfect. I cannot wait to show her to her father.

"Do you have a name?" Claire asks as she tucks me into the blankets. My eyes are starting to droop with sleep, but I am not letting go of my daughter. I am going to hold her all day and all night...and possibly until she is Farli's age.

I nod wearily at Claire. "I think so."

She smiles, not pressing, and squeezes my hand. "So happy for you, my friend. Your daughter is beautiful."

"She is, is she not?" I touch the tiny little horn buds. Everything about her is perfect.

There is a distant shout and more noise at the far end of the vee-lage. Claire gets to her feet, ungainly with her large belly, and gestures at the door. "That might be the hunters returning. If they are, I will send Hemalo your way."

I nod absently. I am too lost in my daughter's beauty, admiring the tiny fingernails at the tip of each small finger. Hemalo should be here, I think. He will want to hold her and welcome her into this world. He needs to hold her to his breast and feel his heart mend, like mine is. "I will never forget your sister," I whisper to my new daughter. "But it does not mean I will love you less. I will give you everything I could not give her...and more."

The privacy screen is flung aside, and Hemalo storms in. His eyes are wild, and he is covered in snow. His normally smooth mane is disheveled. "Asha?"

I put a finger to my lips and then beckon him forward, feeling peaceful and so full of love. "Come greet your daughter."

He falls to his knees where he stands, as if all the strength has left his body. "A girl?"

I nod slowly. We have dreamed of this day for three seasons, but in all of our dreams, we imagined a boy. "I am going to call her Shema," I tell him. "Do you like it?"

He staggers forward, half-crawling to my side, and then sits on his haunches. He stares at her in my arms, wide-eyed. "She is so big."

I chuckle, because she is. She is healthy and stout, my Shema. "Do you want to hold her?"

"More than anything." His voice is hoarse, and his hands tremble as he extends them. I hand her gently over to him, feeling a pang of loss as he takes her from my arms. It dies away the moment I see the sheer joy on his face, the tears shining in his eyes as he gazes down at her. "Hello, Shema," he whispers. "I am your father."

My heart is full.

AUTHOR'S NOTE

The feels. Oh, the feels! I had so many of them when writing this book! I wanted to be respectful to the topic of losing a child, but at the same time, I also didn't want to put readers into a book-long grieving session. It's a fine line to make the story intriguing, romantic, and still hopeful, and I hope I kept you entertained.

One housekeeping note - in a prior story I mentioned that Asha and Hemalo's baby was named Shemalo. In every story after that, the baby was called Hashala. I try to keep vigorous notes on the tribe, but some stuff slips through my fingers. I'm sorry! I'm fixing the earlier book and for clarity's sake, we're going with Hashala. I hope it's not too confusing.

Some of you might ALSO be gnashing your teeth at the fact that I leapt ahead 3 years in the storyline! How can we possibly skip ahead when there's so much going on???? I know, right? I feel like I lost those three years myself! But at the same time...it needed to be done for a few reasons. For one, I couldn't leave Asha wondering and worrying, book after book. Even I'm not THAT cruel. I wanted to show her and Hemalo happy and their arms filled with joy. Second, Farli's story is next, and she has to be adult-aged before we see her with her hero. And her story DOES come next in the timeline, and some important stuff goes down. :)

So, yes, we skipped ahead. By the time Farli's book starts, we're probably going to be 5-6 years post-original crash. You might notice that my people list has now been updated with 'unnamed kit' in several spots, and other couples might have also had more children, but I haven't named it because we haven't ran across it yet in story. I like to hold my cards close to my chest like that! Will we go back and fill in some of the stories in between that we missed out on, like Josie's baby or Liz and Georgie's second births? I do want to, but I'm also trying not to shower you with super-short stories, because let's face it - who wants to read a short story when you can read a full book? But there's still more stuff to cover, so we'll see. I like leaving myself options, even if I don't like leaving the characters.

As for why Claire was given a POV (point of view) in this book — I felt like part of Asha's story was that she'd walled herself off from the tribe and the new human population for so long that she was more alone than ever, and I wanted to give her a friend. I originally thought to include Claire because I wanted to add the holiday fun in, and in my mind, barbarian holidays are narrated by Claire. But! Once I added Claire in, I realized that they would be perfect friends because of Claire's past with Bek and how she hid away from the tribe when she was unhappy. She, of all people, would understand Asha's actions, and I love that she turned into a BFF and defender of our prickliest sa-khui lady.

I'm sure someone out there is wondering why Ereven had no POV then, and well...sometimes people just don't talk to me. That sounds weird and precious even to my own ears, but it's true. When I write, it's like a character is yammering in my ear, and Ereven is just so...chill. He doesn't have much to say because he's a happy, easy guy. Claire was the one with the story, so she was included. I hope that makes sense. Will we ever see a story from Ereven's POV? Just like Ariana and Marlene, once they start speaking to me, I'll write it down. Right now Farli's been shouting pretty loudly (actually for a few books now) so she's next in the lineup.

On one final note, this book is dedicated to all my mamas out there who have gone through the loss of a rainbow baby. So many of you have written to me about this and I hope the story was not too painful to read. I'm thinking of you, ladies. <3

Ruby

THE PEOPLE OF ICE PLANET BARBARIANS

As of the end of Barbarian's Hope

Mated Couples and their kits

Vektal (Vehk-tall) - The chief of the sa-khui. Mated to Georgie.

Georgie – Human woman (and unofficial leader of the human females). Has taken on a dual-leadership role with her mate.

Talie (Tah-lee) – Their baby daughter.

Unnamed Kit - Their 2nd child.

Maylak (May-lack) – Tribe Healer. Mated to Kashrem. Mother of Esha and Makash.

Kashrem (Cash-rehm) - Her mate, also a leather-worker.

Esha (Esh-uh) – Their young daughter.

Makash (Muh-cash) — Their newborn son.

Sevvah (Sev-uh) – Tribe elder, mother to Aehako, Rokan, and Sessah

Oshen (Aw-shen) – Tribe elder, her mate

Sessah (Ses-uh) - Their youngest son

Ereven (Air-uh-ven) Hunter, mated to Claire

Claire – Mated to Ereven, pregnant with a second kit

Erevair - Their first son

Liz – Raahosh's mate and huntress.

Raahosh (Rah-hosh) – Her mate. A hunter and brother to Rukh.

Raashel (Rah-shel) – Their daughter.

Unnamed kit - Their 2nd child.

Stacy – Mated to Pashov. Mother to Pacy, a baby boy.

Pashov (Pah-showv) – son of Kemli and Borran, brother to Farli and Salukh. Mate of Stacy, father to Pacy.

Pacy – Their infant son.

Unnamed kit - Their 2nd child.

Nora – Mate to Dagesh, mother to twins Anna and Elsa.

Dagesh (Dah-zzhesh) (the g sound is swallowed) – Her mate. A hunter.

Anna & Elsa – Their infant twin daughters.

Harlow – Mate to Rukh. Once 'Mechanic' to the Elders' Cave.

Rukh (Rookh) – Former exile and loner. Original name Maarukh. (Mah-rookh). Brother to Raahosh. Mate to Harlow.

Rukhar (Roo-car) – Their infant son.

Megan – Mate to Cashol. Mother to newborn Holvek.

Cashol – (Cash-awl) – Mate to Megan. Hunter. Father to newborn Holvek.

Holvek – (Haul-vehk) – their infant son.

Marlene (Mar-lenn) – Human mate to Zennek. Mother to Zalene. French.

Zennek – (Zehn-eck) – Mate to Marlene. Father to Zalene.

Zalene – (Zah-lenn) – Baby daughter to Marlene and Zennek.

Ariana – Human female. Mate to Zolaya. Mother to Analay.

Zolaya (Zoh-lay-uh) – Hunter and mate to Ariana. Father to Analay.

Analay – (Ah-nuh-lay) – Their infant son.

Tiffany – Human female. Mated to Salukh. Mother to unnamed kit.

Salukh - Salukh (Sah-luke) – Hunter. Son of Kemli and Borran, brother to Farli and Pashov. Father to unnamed kit.

Aehako – (Eye-ha-koh) – Acting leader of the South cave. Mate to Kira, father to Kae. Son of Sevvah and Oshen, brother to Rokan and Sessah.

Kira – Human woman, mate to Aehako, mother of Kae. Was the first to be abducted by aliens and wore an ear-translator for a long time.

Kae (Ki –rhymes with 'fly') – Their newborn daughter.

Kemli – (Kemm-lee) Female elder, mother to Salukh, Pashov and Farli

Borran – (Bore-awn) Her mate, elder

Josie – Human woman. Mated to Haeden and new mother.

Haeden (Hi-den) – Hunter. Previously resonated to Zalah but she died (along with his khui) in the khui-sickness before resonance could be completed. Now mated to Josie. New father.

Unnamed kit - Their 1st child.

Rokan (Row-can) – Oldest son to Sevvah and Oshen. Brother to Aehako and Sessah. Adult male hunter. Now mated to Lila. Has 'sixth' sense.

Lila – Maddie's sister. Hearing impaired. Resonated to Rokan.

Unnamed kit born.

Hassen (Hass-en) – Hunter. Previously exiled. Newly mated to Maddie.

Maddie – Lila's sister. Found in second crash. Newly mated to Hassen.

Unnamed kit born to them.

Asha (Ah-shuh) – Mate to Hemalo. Mother to Hashala (deceased) and Shema, newborn daughter.

Hemalo (Hee-muh-low) - Mate to Asha. Father to Hashala (deceased) and Shema, newborn daughter.

Shema (Shee-muh) - Newborn girl.

Unmated Elders

Drayan (Dry-ann) – Elder.

Drenol (Dree-nowl) – Elder.

Vadren (Vaw-dren) – Elder.

Vaza (Vaw-zhuh) – Widower and elder. Loves to creep on the ladies.

Unmated Females

Farli – (Far-lee) Teenage daughter to Kemli and Borran. Her brothers are Salukh and Pashov. She has a pet dvisti named Chahm-pee (Chompy).

Unmated Hunters

Bek – (BEHK) – Hunter.

Harrec (Hair-ek) – Hunter.

Taushen (Tow – rhymes with cow - shen) – Hunter.

Warrek (War-ehk) – Tribal hunter and teacher. Son to Eklan (now deceased).

ICE PLANET BARBARIANS READING LIST

Are you all caught up on Ice Planet Barbarians? Need a refresher? Click through to borrow or buy and get caught up (or add to your keeper shelf)!

Ice Planet Barbarians – Georgie's Story
Barbarian Alien – Liz's Story
Barbarian Lover – Kira's Story
Barbarian Mine – Harlow's Story
Ice Planet Holiday – Claire's Story (novella)
Barbarian's Prize – Tiffany's Story
Barbarian's Mate – Josie's Story
Having the Barbarian's Baby – Megan's Story (short story)
Ice Ice Babies – Nora's Story (short story)
Barbarian's Touch – Lila's Story
Calm - Maylak's Story
Barbarian's Taming – Maddie's Story
Aftershocks (short story)
Barbarian's Heart – Stacy's Story
Barbarian's Hope - This book!

Next up...
Barbarian's Choice (Farli's Story)

RUBY REC - MARKON'S CLAIM

I love Marina Maddix and her funny, sexy aliens. If you haven't picked this one up yet, why not give it a shot?

MARKON'S CLAIM
Alphas of Thracos Book 2

She wants to do her job. He just wants her.

Ever since being taken in by the Wargs of the Valley, my sole focus has been on curing their fertility problem. I don't care that everyone seems to think I should accept the bite that would transform me into a wolf-like shifter. I have more important things to think about.

Then I meet *him* — the dead-sexy new alpha of the Hill Wargs who can't seem to get enough of my curves. Markon stirs something in me that I've never felt before, and that kind of distraction is the last thing I need. Unfortunately, it's all I can think about.

And now he's pressuring me to become a Warg, too. Something about finding out if I'm his fated mate. Nonsense! Fated mates don't actually exist.

Do they?

WANT MORE?

For more information about upcoming books in the Ice Planet Barbarians, Bear Bites, or any other books by Ruby Dixon, like me on Facebook or subscribe to my new release newsletter.

Thanks for reading!

<3 Ruby

BORING COPYRIGHT STUFF

Made in the USA
Monee, IL
25 September 2023